Over the Dragonwall

By

H.C. Strom
and
Dennis D. Montoya

An Original Publication From H.C. Strom & Dennis D. Montoya

Over the Dragonwall
Copyright © 2015 by Strom & Montoya. All
rights reserved.
ISBN-10: 1-942602-00-6
ISBN-13: 978-1-942602-00-2

First U.S. Paperback Edition, 2015
Printed in the United States of America

SPECIAL THANKS TO

H.P. (the person, not the corp) and *the guys* for their support in this project

Over the Dragonwall

By

H.C. Strom
and
Dennis D. Montoya

Prologue

A call for a hero goes unanswered…

"Why do you haunt my dreams, Hag?"

"I come to gloat, sister. Your time is almost up. The magic of the wall drains away, like water from melting ice. Soon my kind and I will reclaim the southern lands. There is nothing you can do to stop us."

"I will stop you!"

"You are an old swamp witch, sister, nothing more. You have not learned the secrets of power. You cannot save the wall or the souls that it protects. I haunt your dreams to enjoy your despair."

"While I live, you will not breach the wall! Be gone from my slumber, return to your hole, and fester in your hate."

"Ha, why don't you make me leave? Too weak? Like the wall, every year your magic grows weaker, as mine grows stronger. Fear not, dear sister. When I come to rule over your lands, I have no intention of letting you live."

The old witch snapped awake from her nightmare, gasping for breath. The Hag's mocking laugh still echoed in her mind. She rose from her bed. The fire was nearly out, and the hut felt unusually cold. The witch felt very old and alone. She went to the hearth and prodded the ashes in the fireplace. A few coals glowed and sparked, enough to rekindle the fire. She added tinder and branches, till the fire grew.

The Hag was a blunt creature without discipline or imagination. She was driven by the lust for power, revenge, and the petty cruelties visited on the witch's dreams.

It was true. The witch was old, and she did not have all the pieces to rebuild the wall's magic, and so the magic was growing weaker as the years passed. The Hag was right about many, but not all, things concerning the Dragonwall. The witch told herself, "I alone will not strengthen the wall. There were others who could help, some that might not know their part."

The fire warmed the hut; a feeling, for the moment, overtook the witch. She knew what she had to do. Now was the time to cast the bones and see what the future might bring. She took down her bag of sacred bones and laid out the soft pelt of a doe in front of the fire. She played with the bones in her wrinkled hands and cleared her mind's eye. She softly chanted the charm of sight and tossed the bones onto the doe pelt. They rolled and stopped; the symbols showed a possible champion.

Looking past the sacred bones, she drifted into her vision. The hut shimmered and fell away into the ethereal dark abyss. She called out for a champion three times. Her calls went unanswered. She called again to the east, to the west, and to the north. Each time her calls for a champion were unanswered. At the edge of the darkness a small spark shone—not a champion, but a spark that might grow worthy one day.

Away from the swamp, but within reach, the witch's spirit touched a strong heart and a willing mind. It would only take a nudge, and perhaps things could be changed for the Dragonwall. As for the mind she had touched—a lover of knowledge, one with a desire to know—perhaps just a tale would do as the needed nudge ...

One

What has gone before…

Obi always enjoyed the last fire watch just before dawn, giving him extra time to gather his thoughts before starting his morning chores. He added several thin sticks to the embers, nurtured them slowly, till a flame rose into a moderate fire. He put in a few thicker sticks and one small log; the fire began crackling and popping, sending small orange embers into the dark sky. He settled back on his bedroll, admiring the large full moon as it settled into the treetops. The dark sky slowly receded into the west, making way for the sun as it rose into a cloudless blue sky.

Watching the full moon set, Obi's thoughts turned reflective. The moon was full when the group had left the dwarven kingdom of Delvingdeep, heading off to an adventure full of enthusiasm sparked by a bard's tale.

That night the air had been bitter cold, but the inn was warm, and the beer plentiful and hearty. Obi joined Vestos and Delvar, at their favorite watering hole, the Halfway Inn. They sat at their usual table, each with a plate of bread and cheese, and a large tankard of beer. Vestos talked of commerce in the town, the local official gossip, and how to harvest silk.

Obi listened to Vestos's stories with admiration on his keen insight and knowledge, until his attention drifted to someone entering the bar. He wasn't a farmer, merchant, or man-at-arms, but different. The thin man wore shabby clothes and short-cropped hair that looked somehow out of place. He moved around the room, from table to table, not saying a word but admiring the variety of meals. Obi could tell the beggar was hungry. Vestos took notice and made the shabbily clothed man an offer: a silver piece for a grand tale.

Obi thought it cruel, but Vestos had sensed something more to the beggar than his appearance. The disheveled man accepted and produced a small lute to tell his tale. He gave a nod and bow, introducing himself as a humble bard, Fobick. He slowly moved into a clear area near the tables and began a small dance step. He put a finger to his temple and then held it high in the air. "For you gentlemen, I will tell a story of grand adventure that shook the heavens and sealed the fate of men and dragons, The Tale of the Dragonwall."

The bard Fobick began a high-stepping dance and spun lightly on his feet, moving around the room, ensuring he had everyone's attention; even Delvar took notice. Once the entire room turned a watchful eye, the frolicking bard plucked his lute and began to tell his tale.

A thin melody, no more than a pulse, grew into a sweet expression; his voice crisp and clear, he sang his tale of brave men and fierce dragons. A great and heroic battle was fought between the terrible beasts and the combined forces of men, elves, and dwarves.

The Dragon War lasted for many years. In a final battle so climactic and destructive, the gods were moved to protect man by negotiating a peace with the dragons. The dragons would have the lands north of a great river and men the lands to the south. To keep the lands of men, elves, and dwarves separate from the dragons, a great wall was built. No man ventures north of the Dragonwall, lest the dragons again are roused and plague the lands of men. Thus it was that men know of them, but none had ever seen a dragon.

Vestos gladly paid Fobick for his tale. The bard took the coin with a bow, and accepted from the innkeeper a meal of cheese, bread, and wine. He excused himself politely and sat near the fire to enjoy his well-deserved repast. The bard's performance now over, the patrons of the inn turned back to their own conversations.

Obi, Delvar, and Vestos, however, were excited by the tale. The idea that a dragon could be living in the unexplored north was intriguing. What a wonderful thing it would be to see a dragon and bring back the tale for the monastery. Obi said aloud, "To add to the great library's knowledge would be worth so much more than wealth. The knowledge gained would easily surpass the hardships of traveling the wilds."

Delvar scoffed, "For a tale and a rough-drawn picture! Think of the gold, man!"

"Don't forget about the magic!" Vestos wagged a finger in the air excitedly.

As if the matter had already been settled, Delvar declared, "We should go!"

Obi stammered, "I don't know about that."

Vestos raised his tankard. "Yes! We should go! Think of it, Obi. No one from these parts has seen a dragon! If we brought something back, proving we had seen a dragon, we would be famous!"

"Bards would be telling our story!" Delvar took a long pull from his tankard.

"Hear, hear!" Vestos drained his tankard.

Obi didn't know quite what to say, so he tipped up his mug as well. "It was exciting to think about, but …"

Vestos waggled a finger at him now. "But nothing. We should go to see the Dragonwall. We should set off tomorrow."

Obi was excited but nervous too. He knew it was a big journey. "There's only the three of us. How would we manage?"

Delvar waved to the barmaid for more beer and yelled out, "Nonsense! Tark and his buddy Tug would go. They are always saying how they wanted a taste of adventure."

"I know a couple of half-elves," Vestos said brightly. "You remember the ones I told you about? Tannon and his sister, Layna. I think they would go. I will ask them tomorrow."

Obi protested, "Well, in any case, I cannot leave my duties at the monastery. The Sovereign would never allow it."

Delvar sloshed beer at Obi. "Bah! You're just making excuses."

"No I'm not!"

"Ha! I think you are." Vestos laughed. "Drink up, Obi. Old Delvar and I will change your mind yet."

They drained their tankards, while Delvar and Vestos talked of how exciting it would be to see a real dragon. They imagined what a grand tale it would be. How they could find a dragon lair and pluck the finest gems from the treasure hoard to bring back as proof of their adventure. After another tankard they determined they would bring back a scale or a discarded claw as proof of the dragon. After two more tankards they surely would bring back the beast's very head.

By now Obi was warm and happy, and more than a little dizzy. His friends' grand schemes of adventure were wonderful dreams, but he knew, come the morning, he would be back in the great library sweeping the floor. That thought made him a little sad.

"Obi, Obi!" Vestos grabbed Obi roughly on the shoulder. "Promise me …" Vestos swayed, even though he was sitting. "Promise me that you'll ask your blasted Sovereign to go see the dragons."

A promise was something Obi did not take lightly. He could tell Vestos and Delvar were determined, and weighed it against Obi looking foolish in front of the Sovereign. Obi doubted if the Sovereign would ever agree to a drunken errand, but, be it the beer or the bard's tale, Obi made up his mind. "I promise to speak to the Sovereign."

"Hooray!" Delvar shouted, throwing up his arms and promptly falling over backward in his chair. Obi and Vestos burst into laughter, but the innkeeper had had enough. Delvar was helped up, and the three of them were assisted out the door.

The next day found Obi in the library, sweeping. He cursed the original inventor of beer and failed to notice the Sovereign's approach.

"Obi, are you unwell? Your broom seems to be stuck to the floor. It has hardly moved."

Obi stumbled, startled by the Sovereign's voice. "Uh, yes, Sovereign. I mean, no, Sovereign." Obi made a couple feeble passes with the broom.

The Sovereign peered at Obi with a knowing eye. "Have we been studying the art of wine-making this past evening?"

Obi felt his ears glow red. "No, sir."

"Is that so?" the Sovereign said sternly with a slight smile crossing his lips.

Obi glanced up into the Sovereign's face and could see that his master suspected or knew already. He confessed, "It was beer, tankards of beer."

"I would love to know the inspiration for such intense study of brewing. Walk with me and enlighten me."

Obi followed the Sovereign from the library to the courtyard. They passed the fountain and statue of Brother Maynard and continued to the vineyards. Obi related the events of the previous evening. He did his best to recall the bard's tale and the discussion that he had with Delvar and Vestos afterward. To his surprise the Sovereign listened patiently without interrupting.

When Obi had finished, the Sovereign paused, turning to face Obi. "I don't believe I have ever heard of anyone wanting to look upon a dragon just for the sake of seeing a dragon. Most people are interested in gold, magic, and fame. How is it that you have no interest in these things?"

Obi had trouble meeting the Sovereign's eye. "Oh, gold and fame are nice, I suppose. It is just that ..."

"Yes? Go on."

"Well, sir, gold and fame—even magic, I have heard—they don't last. They come to you, and then you pass them on or lose them. But to KNOW, once you know something, sir, it's yours. You can pass it on to others, and yet you never lose it. Surely knowing is worth so much more!"

The Sovereign stared at him intently with a slight smile. "I wonder if you know how wise you are or how inexperienced. I can do nothing about the one thing, but I can fix the other."

"Sir?"

"Obi, tell your friends that I have commanded you to journey to the Dragonwall. Learn of this place and return with the tale, and the knowledge will be added to the library."

This was the last thing Obi had thought the Sovereign would say. "But, sir, it's only a tale, and no doubt they spoke in haste with the courage of beer."

"You will ask them, and, if your friends agree, you will go, and then you will know. The monastery will provide some basic supplies and equipment for your journey." With a nod, the Sovereign retraced his steps.

Obi was stunned, didn't speak.

The Sovereign called back to Obi, "Move along, novice! You have much to do! And mind you, I expect many drawings from this venture!"

Obi had thought the journey north a fool's quest made in haste, with too much beer and festivity. After discussing the quest with his Sovereign of the monastery, he had thought the Sovereign would laugh at their folly, but he didn't. Now Obi realized there was no choice. The Sovereign had ordered the journey. Surprised and dismayed by his master's response, Obi made preparations for his journey.

A week after the Sovereign had told Obi to go to the Dragonwall, Obi and his friends had gathered for their great journey at the town square. A motley crew had formed an adventuring party; each had shown up wearing their adventuring garb—much different from their normal clothing. Vestos changed from his normal breeches to his traveling robes and could be easily mistaken for a pilgrim. He had brought along two others, saying that they might be of help. A brother and sister, Tannon and Layna by name, both were half-elves and were dressed in snug leather armor, showing off their well-muscled bodies. As Delvar had predicted, both Tark and his friend Tug agreed to go. They looked very capable in their armor, wearing long swords. Only Obi was dressed how he was always dressed, in his green monk's robe. They all had packs loaded with supplies; Obi made one last check of his empty journal and his writing quills before he shouldered his heavy pack.

The bard Fobick had stated with conviction that dragons existed many miles north of Delvingdeep, beyond the Dragonwall. He said, if they truly wanted to see dragons, then they merely had to place one foot in front of the other and go.

So the journey north began.

Two

I thought it would be a short walk…

The last cold days of winter were coming to an end. Spring showers awaken the trees and shrubbery as new foliage emerges from the once frozen soil. A variety of birds fill the air with lyrical calls and melodies. A breeze carries the aroma of pine, wet grass and blooming wild flowers. The group had been several days into their journey, and their schedules were more routine now. Obi stoked the fire and began to tidy up around camp. He rolled up his bedroll and secured it to his pack, and then he checked his crossbow and counted his bolts—a dozen plus three. He still had a week of rations, a water skin, and three red apples he had been saving since the journey began. He checked the writing book that the Sovereign had given Obi to document his travels. He wrapped it tightly in a leather binding. He wondered what adventures the book would hold and looked forward to retelling his tale to the Sovereign.

Obi put a pot of water over the fire to boil. Vestos always did enjoy a bit of tea in the morning. He noticed that Vestos's small cauldron was near the fire as well. Obi lifted the lid and saw that Vestos had prepared this morning's breakfast the night before. He had filled the small pot with water and wheat grain, to allow the grain to soak and soften overnight. This morning, as was his custom, Vestos would make morning gruel for the group. It wasn't the best breakfast, but, as long as Vestos had his spices and herbs, it was quite satisfying. The hot gruel was filling and would keep hunger at bay until the evening meal.

The members of the group were beginning to stir. Obi moved the little cauldron closer to the fire, so it could heat. The sun had taken the sky, thrusting bright rays through the morning mist.

Vestos was up first. He stood in his rumpled robe and stretched out the kinks in his tall frame. Mumbling a morning greeting to Obi, he stumbled off into the woods to answer the call of nature. Tannon was up a moment later. He checked on his sister and, in his half-elf way, looked like he had been up for hours. Tannon placed his warm blanket on top of her. Layna snuggled down under the watchful eye of her great owl, Swiftwing. Tug abruptly sat up out of his bedroll, farted, and stomped off into the woods, just as Vestos was coming back.

Obi noticed that Delvar had cracked open an eye, then closed it again, shifting only enough to warm his feet by the fire. Obi was struck by the sudden thought that Delvar would not get up until there was a larger audience to see the event.

Vestos busied himself around the fire, getting the cauldron just so and checking the tea. He went to his pack, pulling out a cloth bag of herbs and his tin drinking cup. Obi noted that the cloth bag was nearly empty.

Tark and Layna were up. They picked up their gear, securing their bedrolls and helping themselves to a plate of gruel.

Delvar made a loud yawn, before quickly rolling out of his bed, and stood erect. He stretched, which was composed of several flexing poses showing off his broad shoulders, thick arms, and hairy chest. Ending his performance with a brisk hand rub, Delvar asked, "What's for breakfast?"

With an air of annoyance Layna said, "Gruel of course."

Tannon shot Delvar a dark look. "Did you misplace your shirt this morning?"

Delvar rolled his hand across his mustache and then his fingers through his hair. "My shirt was here a minute ago."

Everyone ignored his banter, except for Layna, who stole subtle glances at him. Obi wanted to cheer and clap for such a performance but resisted the urge.

Delvar pulled out a red silk shirt from his bedroll and began a well-rehearsed stretching event to put on his shirt. He glanced at Layna. "For the life of me, I don't know how that shirt fell off."

Layna smiled broadly and then quickly hid her interest behind a look of annoyance.

Obi thought she had done that for Tannon's benefit. Obi had considered mimicking Delvar's stretching and posing, but, without the fuzzy chest, he would not have given the same performance.

Tug took a large mouthful of gruel and swallowed hard. "Damn, Vestos. You make that gruel good enough to eat."

Vestos grinned. "Glad you like it. The trick is in the ratio. You get that off, and it becomes too tart or too bitter. When we get to town, a bit of browned butter would do nicely."

Tug ignored him and took a second helping of gruel.

Swiftwing landed on Layna's outstretched hand. She rubbed its chest, making a soft cooing sound. "Are you hungry, Swiftwing? Yes, you are."

Swiftwing made a loud clicking noise and let out a quiet "Hoo-hoo."

Layna pulled a piece of bread from a pocket and gave it to her owl. She ate it quickly. "Perhaps today we will find you something to eat besides hard bread."

Tark finished his gruel and put his spoon into his pack. "The way I figure it, going through the swamp will save us two or three days."

Layna pulled out a small loaf of bread, tearing off pieces and putting them into her pocket, replenishing her supply. She fed a few more bites to Swiftwing. "The snowpack is still frozen in the area. Crossing the swamp should be easy this time of year."

Tark arranged his armor pieces. "So it is agreed. We go through the swamp."

Vestos made a face. "The swamp is wet. What about firewood? It will make for a cold night and a cold breakfast."

Obi pulled a thin leather cord from his pocket. "I can gather firewood as we go, using this strap to wrap up the bundle. In the monastery everyone carries a strap like this."

Tug was dressed in his armor too and made a face. "Obi, you are always pulling something out of your pockets. What else do you have in those robes?"

Obi ignored him.

Donning his gray scale armor, Tark grumbled, "I don't mind trudging through the water, but I am getting sick of this hardtack and stale cheese for dinner. I would give ten silver crowns for a hot meal."

Obi liked the idea of a hot meal, but there was not an inn for several days' walk.

Layna sat on her pack, brushing her hair. She turned quickly. Her red-rimmed eyes dancing with mischief, she giggled. "I can summon up food for us, especially in the swamp."

Tark's ears perked up, along with several others among the group. "How are you going to do that?"

Layna gave a somber nod. "With a little magic, food will drop from the sky."

Tark shook his head. "Will it rain food? I think you have been in the sun too long."

She scratched Swiftwing's chest, making a cooing sound, before letting her take to the air, and turned back to Tark. "I will make you a wager that I can get a better meal than you by the end of the day. Let's say, five copper?"

Tannon choked out a cough. "Layna! You shouldn't tease these men."

Layna shot Tannon a stare. "I know what I am doing." Then she faced Tark. "Do we have a wager?"

Tark looked at Tannon and back to Layna. "Let's make it a silver crown."

Her mischievous grin didn't fade. Layna pulled open her pack, undid a small bag, and retrieved a sliver coin.

Tannon shook his head. "Layna, don't! We need that silver."

Layna hushed him before turning back to Tark. "Deal!"

Tark held out his hand. "Shake on it, and the deal is sealed, but the winner has to cook dinner."

Layna nodded, gripping his large hand and shaking vigorously, smiling up at him. "You are going to owe me a silver piece."

Tark shrugged. "We will see when the food rains from the sky."

Vestos rolled out a small pouch. "I will put a silver crown on Layna. She's a clever one."

Tark smiled. "I will take that wager. Any others?"

Delvar swirled his cloak and produced a silver piece. "The smallest I have, if you're willing to take my small wager on Layna."

Tark took the silver. "Anyone else?"

Vestos nudged Obi. "When it comes to betting, you always bet on magic!"

Obi could not imagine what kind of magic Layna might possess. She had not had any claim of magic or tricks. All she had done since the trip began was fight with Tannon and play with her owl. In the recent days Obi had noticed her looking at Delvar when no one was watching. Obi had watched her eyes carefully; her gaze would be squarely fixed on Tark or another of the party, but, when she thought no one was watching, she would steal glances at Delvar.

Vestos nudged him again. "Quick, isn't she?"

Obi nodded in agreement, not taking his eyes off the wagering.

Tug cleaned up his plate and put it away. "Everyone knows the smart silver is on Tark. I will wager a silver crown on him."

Vestos, nodding, said, "Good, good. I will take that bet."

Obi bent close to Vestos. "Didn't you just wager on Layna and all that about magic?"

Vestos nodded. "Right you are! I bet silver on both. This way, I get to participate in the fun, and, whoever wins, I keep all of my silver."

Obi paused a moment. "Now who is the clever one?"

Vestos gave him a sly grin and a wink.

Layna's red-rimmed eyes flashed with mischief and asked, "What would you like to eat? Snake, bird, or rabbit?"

Tark rubbed his chin whiskers before answering, "Rabbit is good. A few rabbit skins will make a good helmet liner or a pair of gloves."

Layna winked at him. "Rabbit it is."

Tark gave a grin and rubbed his belly. "Did everyone bet against me?"

Vestos smiled at him. "Not so much as betting against you, just betting on Layna. She is using magic, and you must side with magic. Besides, she is prettier than you."

Tannon deliberately stepped in between Vestos and Layna, blocking his view, and Tannon pulled her close. "Layna, we can't afford to lose that silver. We don't have that much."

She leaned in and kissed his cheek. "Always the worrier. Don't you trust my magic?"

Tannon rolled his eyes. "What magic? I know you have lived with the druids. Do you really have magic?"

She winked at him and raised her eyebrows toward Swiftwing.

Tannon rolled his eyes. "Oh, you are talking about those tricks you teach your owl?"

"They are not tricks. I have been training Swiftwing. She is a good hunter."

Tannon threw up his hands. "You're betting on your bird to get a rabbit?"

Layna smiled at him. "It will be all right. It is only silver, and I tried for five copper, remember? But Tark wanted to bully me. I won't be bullied by anyone, not even by you, little brother."

Tannon protested, but Layna's sharp look stopped him. Layna moved across the camp to Tark, holding up another silver piece. "Tark, you want to make it two silver crowns?"

Tark shook his head. "Everyone thinks you're going to beat me anyway. Still I will take your wager. The winner buys the first round at Midreach. We are going to Midreach, or was it Farreach?"

Tug made a face. "I bet on you, and it was Midreach."

Vestos picked up his spear and donned his pack. "That bard was very specific about Midreach. Although, when he said it, it sounded like it would be a short journey."

Tug, Tannon, and Obi nodded in agreement.

Tark donned his scale gloves and backpack. He patted his long sword secured to his belt and checked the surrounding area for anything he might have dropped. "Obi, you're going to gather firewood as we go?"

Obi held out his long leather strap with a loop on it. He picked up a few long branches and secured them with his cord. "I will start right now, and Tannon said he would help me. If that load gets heavy, we will switch off."

Tark smiled at him. "Good. Who will take point?"

Delvar rolled his hands across his mustache and flared his cloak. "I can take point, and everyone can follow me. I am as sure-footed as the best thief."

Layna was quick to raise her hand. "I will help you. I am familiar with the swamp."

Tark counted the party members. "Okay, good. We need someone to trail behind to be used as an anchor, so we will stay on course."

Tannon, now pouting, said, "Me. I will trail behind. Apparently my sister doesn't listen to me anymore."

Delvar and Layna led the way; the party set off in the morning sun.

Obi tried to reassure Layna's brother. "Tannon, here in the woods, trouble is more likely to come to the city-born Delvar than your sister."

Tannon brought up the rear. "Yes, but I tend to worry. Layna is impulsive and too trusting. I will keep an eye on her to keep her out of trouble."

Three

What do you mean, we have to sleep in the swamp?

The party traveled down a path and stopped at the edge of a valley. Obi stood on tiptoes for a better look. He could see rows of large trees rimming the valley's edge and dark spots showing remnants of an old forest fire.

Layna and Delvar discussed the best way to navigate the swamp. Delvar pushed for speed in crossing the swamp, while Layna argued for caution. After several minutes Tark grew impatient and stopped the arguing. He looked at Delvar and Layna, and made a wide sweep of his hand and a slight bow, indicating they should lead on. Layna giggled and skipped down the trail.

Obi could see the basin was littered with small streams that zigzagged their way through the valley, forming ponds. Scattered along the bottom of the valley stood rolling hills with humps of tall shrubs and trees, but none were as large as those in the forest they were leaving. He scratched his head. "Not much shade. I think it is going to be hot down there."

Vestos stretched his neck, looking at the marsh, then back to the trees. "I think you are quite correct, quite hot and humid. It makes me thankful for one thing. I am glad I'm not wearing that metal armor!" Vestos let out a loud belly laugh at his own joke.

Tug took notice of the remark. He picked up a small rock, throwing it at Vestos. The rock whizzed past him. Vestos jumped back. "No offense intended."

Tug gave him a surly grin, dropping the remaining stones.

Obi did not envy Tark and Tug in their heavy metal armor. Obi was thankful his robes were not hot or cold, but they always felt normal. The trees of the swamp looked water-soaked compared to the ones here. "Before we get into that marsh, I think everyone should grab a walking stick. It will be handy for checking the bottom of pools, and we can burn the sticks when we make camp."

Delvar and Tark declined, stating they would need their hands free in case of trouble. Obi suspected Tark always talked with his hands, and a staff might cause him to stutter. The others began searching for suitable walking sticks.

Tug found a stick nearly as tall as himself. He quickly made short stabbing motions, as if he were fishing with a spear. The others made an attempt to find theirs.

Obi found a broad pole taller than Vestos, much longer than an average walking stick. He rolled it across his hands checking the weight. The pole reminded him of the staffs he had trained with at the monastery. He tested it for weak points, in case he needed to use it in a fight. He doubted it would last longer than a few heavy strikes before splintering. The pole was not of staff quality, but it would be a good walking stick and later added to a fire.

Tug nodded his approval proudly, making more stabbing motions with his makeshift spear.

It seemed like they had been walking for hours over clumps of grass, tall weeds, wildflowers, and reeds. A pebble had made its way into Obi's boot; with each step it would roll this way and that way, sometimes giving him a sharp pinch. He wiggled his toes and kicked his boot, and the pebble would seem to go away for a few steps just to roll around and poke his foot again. He made up his mind—at the next rest stop he would shake out his boot.

Obi watched Layna as she led Delvar around the swamp. She would make hand signals to him, but Obi doubted if Delvar knew what she meant. Given Layna's mischievous nature, Obi wondered if she was making random hand signals just to tease Delvar.

Layna raised her hands high above her head, then low again, making pushing-away motions, then a circling gesture above her head. Delvar shrugged in bewilderment.

Layna pointed to the path rimming the long edge of the burned area. The space wasn't very wide, but the underbrush was thicker, and the ground was drier. Delvar took Layna's advice and headed toward the rise.

They trudged over a hump of shrubs and moved around a large boggy area, where Delvar began sinking into the marsh. He waved for the party to stop, as he and Layna moved back and forth, making their way past a second outcropping of thin trees and a stagnant patch of water, before signaling for the rest of their party to continue.

Layna indicated to circle to the right, until they stood on the edge of a shallow stream.

Vestos dipped a hand in and, tasting the water, loudly announced, "It's fresh and cold." He reached for his water skin and filled it. Taking a long drink, he let out a loud, satisfied sigh.

The rest of the group did the same, getting a good drink and topping off their own water skins. Tug and Tark splashed water on their faces and into their hair to cool themselves.

Delvar was more reserved, drank just as deeply, then dampened a fine silk kerchief and dabbed the sweat from his forehead and the back of his neck.

Vestos asked Obi, "What have you put in your writing book so far on our journey?"

Obi hadn't drawn a single image or written down one word. He wanted the book to be exceptional and interesting but was afraid of the "What ifs." There was so much he didn't know: What if it wasn't good? What if someone laughed at him? What if the Sovereign didn't like the book? Obi found it difficult to know where to start. Obi shook his head. "I was saving it for when we see the Dragonwall."

Vestos gave him a knowing look. "What if there are no dragons or no Dragonwall? You went on the adventure and have nothing to show for it. What would your master say about that?"

Obi knew Vestos was right. Obi would start at the beginning, when they had first encountered the bard. Obi started writing down what he could recall from Bard Fobick, and who was there, and traveling through the forest and now the swamp. But he needed something more. He needed a picture of the people with him. But who would be first? And what if they didn't like the drawing? Obi thought it foolish of himself. He made up his mind; he would draw and write anyway, and realized the writing book wouldn't be perfect, but it would be honest. Since Vestos and Delvar were with him when the journey began, he would draw them first.

Vestos stood half a head taller than Delvar, and Vestos's pilgrim attire did a good job in hiding his girth. He was quick to laugh, and was always doting on his herbs and spices. What Obi found most incredible about this friend was his knowledge; he had a reserve of knowledge on many subjects, ranging from merchant commerce to military tactics. Obi wanted to capture Vestos's essence in a drawing, but found capturing his attitude was difficult, until Obi pulled out a piece of charcoal, made some light sketches. He drew Vestos with his herb bag, heating morning gruel. Once Obi was satisfied, he turned the page and set his eye on Delvar.

Obi watched Delvar and Tark discuss the best way to proceed through the swamp. Delvar stood almost a head taller than Tark, with large muscles enhanced by his tight-fitting shirt. He had curly brown hair and a sparkle in his eye. Obi thought, in a fair fight, Delvar would easily overmatch Tark with his size, but Obi tempered that assumption by what the Sovereign had said: bigger in size doesn't always mean winning. Obi suspected that Tark's experience and fury might tip the scales in his favor. Tark was shorter and leaner, and seemed to possess a tempered resilience from serving in the militia. Tark had a darker complexion with piercing blue eyes that seemed to look directly into Obi's soul. Tark didn't smile often and always seemed to worry about the party more than himself. Obi tried to capture the subtle tones of Delvar's courtly mannerisms and Tark's rugged charisma. Obi made a few sketches of the two men poised, looking down the valley.

Seeing everyone had satisfied their thirst, Layna hopped over the little stream and headed into the marsh, with Delvar following closely.

Tark urged everyone to stay close together in the tall grass; no one disagreed. The grass was already to Obi's thigh and grew taller with each step.

Vestos took a long look around and nudged Obi. "For a marsh it doesn't seem that unpleasant of a place. The sun is warm, and it is still early in the season, so there are not too many bugs."

Obi thought so too; he had expected the swamp to be wetter. "The ground seems solid, but this grass is thick and scratchy."

Vestos used his spear to push aside the grass. "It's getting taller, and Layna is getting harder to see. I am off to follow her trail."

Swiftwing rose out from the tall grass, moving silently across the sky.

Vestos startled, called out, "Whoa! Blasted bird gave me a fright. Now we will see if it rains rabbits."

Obi absently followed Vestos's trail, trudging through the grass, occasionally coming to a small rivulet of running water to be jumped over. They had crossed countless rivulets and two moderate-size streams before someone called for a break.

Wasting no time, Obi pulled out his sketchbook and quickly started sketching Tug. He was taller than Tark, but not as tall as Delvar. He had thick arms and looked capable in any situation. He had a way about him where he could size up a situation in moments, combined with an ornery streak. Earlier in the day, when Vestos had made a joke about being happy he was not wearing their heavy armor, Tug had taken offense and had thrown a rock at Vestos. Tug didn't seem angry—just that he doesn't back down from anything. Obi tried to capture Tug's willful nature, giving him a stern look with just a hint of a smile.

Obi put away his book, and the party kept moving into the swamp. The sun climbed in the sky, and it became hot and humid. The pebble in Obi's boot seemed to lodge itself to one side and was no longer pinching him.

The swamp leveled off, and the ground became spongier and wetter. The grass grew in tall clumps with cattails scattered though the patches. Looking down on the valley, Obi thought he would be able to see a long ways, but tall grasses and rolling hills made it difficult to see more than ten paces. Obi stepped into a rivulet. Annoyingly cold water ran through his boots.

Vestos made a face. "I am reconsidering my first estimation of the swamp being a nice place. It is too hot for my liking."

Layna and Delvar seem to have reached the same conclusion. They headed for one of the larger patches of brush that they had seen earlier. In short order the little group had gathered at the edge of a small rise covered in trees. Layna wiped the perspiration from her face.

Obi was surprised by the walking stick in Tark's hand. He and Delvar had been quite adamant about not taking one. Obi asked, "I thought you needed your hands free?"

Tark stammered out, "Ah, well … you know, there, ah, doesn't seem to be anything here to worry about. And it was a good idea." He shifted uneasily and pointed out a break in the foliage. "Look here. Maybe we can get through the brush and to drier ground."

The small opening in the thick brush was filled with dried grass, making it little more than a hole. Tug pulled out his heavy-bladed short sword and quickly cut a path that led them to a raised area. After a few feet the brush turned to densely grown elder trees with an opening wide enough for everyone to find a place to sit down. It was cooler in the shade, but the air was still heavy and thick without a breeze.

Vestos pulled out his water skin, taking a large gulp of water. "I do not want to camp in the swamp. No place to lie down and stretch out."

Obi found a small spot to sit, nuzzled against a few tiny saplings. It was more comfortable than he had thought possible. It felt good to get off his feet. He pulled off his pack, undid his boot, shook out two small pebbles, and put it back on. He dug through his pack and withdrew three red apples and a silver knife. He chopped the apples in half, cut out the core, and handed them to the party.

Vestos took a large bite of apple. "Obi, is there not enough for you?"

Obi was hungry, but there were only six halves and seven party members; he had hoped no one would notice but was not surprised Vestos had made the comment. The monastery had raised Obi to be humble. It was better to give to the party than to himself. He pulled out a small loaf of bread, and began cutting up pieces of it and handing them out. He lied, "I am not hungry."

Vestos gave him a doubtful look.

The look made Obi feel exposed, and he wondered if Vestos could see he was lying. Obi shrugged and hoped that Vestos wouldn't say anything.

Vestos dabbed a rag across his sweaty face and neck, and finished his snack. "Damn good apple. I didn't think we had any more."

Obi had been saving the apples since their journey had begun, keeping them safe from bruising, but thought one more day in this heat and the apples would surely rot. He pulled out a second loaf. "Those were the last. Would anyone like more bread?"

Tug took a piece, and so did Delvar. Layna quietly ate her apple and stared up at the sky, seemingly unaware of the rest of the party.

Obi pulled out his sketchbook and began sketching the brother and sister. The siblings were the same height and complexion. Layna's hair was darker than Tannon's with streaks of blond highlights. Their tight-fitting leather armor made their toned physiques stand out. Obi drew Layna fighting with Tannon and then drew her silhouette with Swiftwing perched upon her outstretched arm.

When everyone had eaten their snack, Obi put the rest of the loaf into his pack and secured the silver knife in its pouch.

Vestos studied the sky. "We are not traveling as fast as I thought."

Tark licked his fingers and drank deeply from his water skin. "We might have to camp in this swamp after all. Layna, Delvar, start looking for a suitable campsite."

Tug stood up, visibly irritated, even more than usual. "What the hell! I do not want to sleep in the swamp. I say we push on into the night, if we have to."

Obi could see Tug was frustrated and his tone was growing angrier. Obi had also hoped they would not have to camp in the swamp and was wondering what Tug would do if they had to stay the night.

Vestos cleared his throat. "Layna told me that the swamp is dangerous, and animals feed at night. Go ahead and tell them, Layna, what you told me about the swamp."

She pulled her eyes from the sky. "All sorts of things hunt at night—snakes, alligators, rats, not to mention a muddy bog during the day can be seen, but, at night, a bog becomes very dangerous."

Obi didn't like the idea of creatures out at night. He imagined large spiders crawling over them as they slept. Why didn't she mention the crawlies before they were halfway through the swamp? He felt his hands tremble. He watched the others for signs of nervousness. No one else looked concerned, except Tug, who looked angry.

Tark said, "Layna, you make a good point. We are about halfway through the swamp, perhaps less. We could turn back and go around. It would put us back a day, plus three more to travel around the swamp."

"No. With Delvar's help, I can find wetter trails with shallow marshes that we can cross to save time instead of looking for drier land," Layna said.

Delvar flared his cloak and took a long confident stride into the pool of water. The boggy bottom gave way to thick silt, and he sank to his waist. He struggled to maintain his balance and rocked to a stop.

"If you would have taken a walking stick, you could have checked the bottom of that pool." Layna giggled.

Everyone laughed.

Delvar tried to wrench out his front leg; it held. He tried again. He waved his arms wildly to catch his balance. Layna moved closer, but kept her feet planted on the drier ground and handed Delvar her walking stick. Using the staff like a rope, Delvar pulled himself out the bog.

Obi pulled out his writing book and touched up Layna's picture.

Delvar brushed the silt and mud off his boots, and shook out his fouled cloak. He used his dagger to scrap mud from his breeches, stomped his feet to remove the excess, but his doused enthusiasm shone through his wet clothes.

Curious about what Obi was drawing, Layna came close and looked over his shoulder to examine her portrait. After a few minutes she asked, "Can you make my hair longer?"

Obi thought for a moment and carefully made sure the contours matched the rest of the drawing. He showed her; Layna gave her approval.

Obi had the first part of the expedition in his journal and considered what other wonders would fill its pages. He wrapped up the journal and tucked it neatly in his pack. A moment later Tark called for Layna and Delvar to take point. The party moved forward through the swampy area into the taller grass. The rolling hills made Obi think they were at the bottom of the swamp and were, at last, starting out the other side.

Four

Did you hear that?

The party marched along the swamp, moving past tall reeds, grasses, and clumps of trees. The wind had stopped blowing, and the air grew hot. Something moved, catching Obi's eye; a dark object moved fast over the tall grass. A chill crossed Obi, making the small hairs on his neck rise. Obi was certain he had seen something but couldn't tell what it was. He looked again, waiting for it to rise up, but the sunset made it difficult to see beyond the bright sun and the dark shadows. He moved to catch up to Vestos, when he caught sight of the dark, bobbing shade. He tried to dismiss it as something caught in the wind, but there was no wind. The sun's glare made it difficult to tell what it was, except it was fast—and silent. It raced across the top of the grass, heading toward their party, straight at Tark.

Obi had to warn Tark. Obi's crossbow was slung over his back, but the dark object would be on Tark before Obi could pull it out. He called out, "Tark! Watch out!"

Tark spun on his heels. His hand sped to unsheathe his blade. A brown flash, bobbing its way among the grass, was weaving low to the ground. A brown bag shot toward Tark, striking him in the chest. Whoop! Tark jumped and yelled out, "Bloody hell!"

The bag fell to the ground.

Tark jerked his sword free, trying to see what was thrown at him. Layna's owl, Swiftwing, circled the party, letting out a piercing screech, and darted back toward the setting sun.

Tark looked at the bag. It wasn't a bag at all but a large jackrabbit.

"That rabbit fell from the sky!" Tug let out a howling laugh.

A mighty roar of laughter erupted from the party.

Tark laughed, and his smile didn't fade. "Good job, Layna. Food from the sky!"

Layna hefted the rabbit and said, "If there are no objections, I will make rabbit stew tonight."

Tark shook his head, looking at the rabbit. "I prefer my meat roasted."

Tug and Delvar nodded in agreement.

Layna pointed out, "Since she provided the dinner, Swiftwing gets her favorite parts. Roast rabbit is good, but this would hardly be a mouthful among the seven of us, eight counting Swiftwing. Should I make the stew?"

The wager settled, Tark held out two silver crowns to Layna. "Yes, stew makes sense. Well done, Layna. You won the bet fair and square."

She grinned. "I believe our bet called for RABBITS, not one rabbit."

Tark stopped momentarily, then brightened. "Why so it did!" Ignoring Tannon's groan of frustration, Tark tossed the coins into the air and deftly caught them. He turned away to join Tug.

In a low voice Tannon said, "Layna, you won the bet fair enough! Why take more chances with our silver?"

She cupped Tannon's cheek and explained, "When betting with friends, it is always best to win in a way where everyone wins. Another rabbit or two and we will all have a large dinner with no hard feelings to the silver I won."

Tannon's brow furrowed, as he considered her statement. He winced and said, "You don't know that Swiftwing will get another rabbit."

"Trust me, brother. I have seen rabbit signs everywhere. We may yet have roasted rabbits!"

Tannon scowled for a moment but was unable to hold the frown when Layna stuck out her lower lip in a mock pout. Tannon threw up his hands and mumbled a short prayer for strength and finally smiled at Layna, letting her know he wasn't really angry.

Obi watched Vestos butcher the rabbit, admiring his skill with a blade. In short order Vestos finished cleaning the rabbit and bundled it in its own skin. He tied the bundle to a stick, where he had also put the liver and choice bits in a pouch, before putting it all across one shoulder.

The shadows had stretched out, and Obi suspected, in an hour or less, it would be dusk. He wished Layna would not have told him of the night creatures. Now he couldn't help but think of the snakes and alligators crawling over him as he slept. He wondered if he could sleep standing up.

Every step produced a small pool of water around their well-soaked boots. Delvar picked up the pace. Although he did not complain, his irritation with the swamp showed in the way he shook the mud from his boots and frowned at the soiled condition of his cloak. Delvar stopped and raised his hand and sniffed the air. "I believe I smell a cook fire. Perhaps there is a town or village nearby." Delvar surged ahead.

Layna tugged at his sleeve. "Hold on, Delvar! We cannot assume a friendly greeting at every campfire."

Delvar stood straight. "My dear miss, I feel that no one would live in this swamp without a purpose, and people with a purpose can be talked to and negotiated with. A village is what we are headed for, and they will welcome our coin."

Layna cautioned, "We are in the swamp. They could be bandits, hiding out from the law."

He swayed his cloak in a nervous gesture. "Perhaps a reasonable amount of caution is warranted. Still, anyone who lives here will know the area better than we do. They would know where the nearest tavern is." Eager to get moving, Delvar turned to continue hiking.

"Wait a moment! Wait a moment! There is a tall and stout tree right over there." Layna said, "Tannon could climb that and perhaps see the smoke. It would at least give us the right direction to take."

Delvar made a slight bow and sweep of his hand. "An excellent notion! Lead on, Tannon."

Tannon came forward, carefully picking his way to the tree Layna had pointed out.

Obi noticed that Tannon was watchful of where he planted his feet, marking a sharp contrast between the flashy Delvar and the competent half-elf.

Tannon stood at the base of a heavily overgrown tree. With a glance back, he began to climb. He had no trouble finding branches that would support his light muscular frame, but he did struggle with the dense foliage and numerous dead branches, snapping and cracking as he pulled himself up through the foliage. Several small dark birds were disturbed from their roost, leaving their violated space in shrill protest. Tannon climbed till he was perhaps three times the height of Vestos. Hanging by one hand with his feet braced against the trunk, like a sailor on a mast, he scanned the swamp.

Delvar shaded his eyes, looking upward. "What do you see?"

Tannon called down, "You have a good nose for a cook fire, Delvar. We are coming to a larger stream. It runs east to west across our path. There is a small lake. That is where the smoke is coming from."

Delvar patted his stomach. "An empty belly and wet feet will do that to you."

Tannon descended the tree. Tark gave him a slap on the back. "Excellent! Let us hope for a dry shelter and a welcome fire."

Delvar continued, "Let's go. We have a lot of ground to cover before it gets dark."

Delvar led the way with Tug just behind, his short sword drawn. Delvar moved even more carelessly now, so eager was he to find his supposed "village."

The sun was just about to touch the treetops when Delvar came to a break in the tall grasses. In the distance, a low growl rumbled, turning into a solitary howl. Delvar called out, "Did you hear that howl? I haven't heard anything like it."

Obi didn't hear the howl. All he had heard for most of the day was the sloshing water. He cupped his hands to his ears. "I hear nothing. Anyone else? What did it sound like?"

Delvar waved a hand at him to be quiet. Everyone stood, listening for any sound; only their light breathing could be heard.

Obi whispered, "What did it sound like?"

Delvar whispered back, "It was quite disturbing. It was a growling howl. I haven't heard anything like it."

Obi could feel his heartbeat quicken, and he wished he was back at the monastery. "Perhaps we should get to that village."

Tark raised his hand to get everyone's attention, then motioned forward, to get the party moving.

Without another word, Delvar pushed forward through the grass, slogging through a small boggy area, a reed patch, and past a large muddy pond of croaking frogs.

In less than a bow's range, the group exited the field of tall grass and stood on the edge of a wide pond. The pond was narrow where they stood but got larger to the east. In the center a small island rose from the water. At the highest point of the island stood a modest stone hut with a sod roof. A small stone chimney poked up from the far side of the roof. Beyond the hut was another building, longer and narrower than the first. It was built differently, having a low stone foundation and log walls, with no windows. The large double doors at the narrow end gave the impression of a barn. Between the two buildings was an open fire pit. On the spit, a large boar lay roasting over the fire.

Delvar rubbed his stomach. "That boar smells so dang good."

Obi's mouth began to water.

Tug motioned across the water and said, "There is a dock over there and a boat."

Obi had missed the dock completely, focusing on his hunger more than what was around him. Not far from the two buildings, built into the lake, was a small wooden dock. On the shore, a small dugout canoe had been partially pulled from the water.

Everyone paused for a moment, before Layna praised, "Good eyes, Tug. That island might prove to be a dry campsite, but we will get wet crossing here."

Tug thumped on his chest plate. "One of you wearing clothes should go retrieve the boat."

Obi knew what Tug meant. He wanted Obi or Vestos to swim across and retrieve the boat. Obi suspected that Vestos didn't know how to swim, so it would be up to Obi. Vestos looked like he would say something, but any rebuke would cause Tug to retaliate. Obi thought Tug would toss rocks at Vestos or push him into the lake. Obi just hoped the lake didn't have any leeches. Flinging his pack to Delvar, he took off his robes. "I will go. Just keep my pack dry, and I will swim over and get it."

Vestos nodded a silent thank-you.

Obi stripped off his belt, all his robes, and boots. He stood at the edge of the lake, his lean physique and muscular legs evident to all.

Tannon shielded his sister from Obi's nakedness. She peeked around him, giggling. "He is muscular."

"No, Layna, he is naked."

Layna laughed. "I know."

"Layna!" Tannon scolded.

She let out a loud cackling laugh and in a scratchy voice said, "Oh, I like those buns!"

The laugh made Tannon stop and look her. "Layna, was that you?"

Layna shook her head and pointed. "That cackle wasn't me. It was her."

Behind Layna stood a woman of considerable age, her straggly long black hair streaked with gray. Her face was wrinkled about a large nose and big eyes and a wicked-looking smile, showing her yellowing teeth. She stared at Obi's muscular frame. "I do like those buns!"

Obi jumped, turned, and crouched down, trying to hide his genitals.

Five

Obi has a girlfriend

The old woman intently watched as Obi retrieved his clothing from Delvar and began to dress. Once he had on his robes, the old woman turned away. "Now that all the good parts are covered, how did you end up on my doorstep?"

"Your doorstep?" Delvar repeated.

She looked directly at him and pointed to the island. "Yes, this is Majora's Island. I should know. I am Majora."

Delvar gave a courtly bow. "We are travelers headed to Midreach, a town on the Dragonwall. More pressing, we are looking for a dry campsite."

She gave a crooked grin. "Do you know you're in the swamp? There are not many dry places here."

Delvar gave a broad smile. "We wanted to cross the swamp before nightfall, but we ran out of light. Perhaps we could camp on your island?"

Majora smiled and giggled. "Visitors. I never get visitors. I suppose you can stay in the barn."

Delvar gave another bow, deeper than the first. "Thank you, madam."

She winked at Obi. "You can stay in the house!"

Obi felt like a fly caught in a web, with her being the spider, and wondered what things she would do to him. He felt his face flush; he wanted to say something, but his mouth just opened and closed.

Majora let out a loud cackling laugh. "Speechless! You should see your face! Ha! I wouldn't want to corrupt your youth, child. We would do things that would curl your toes and would spoil you for any other woman."

Laughter erupted from the party, everyone except Layna, who looked a little sadly at him.

Embarrassment overwhelmed him; Obi could not believe what Majora was saying. He couldn't help but think about what she would do to make his toes curl. His ears turned bright red. He wanted to say something to get the attention off him, but he could only think of his toes curling. He bit his lip.

Majora threw her head back, letting out a loud cackle, and playfully slapped Obi across the back. "I love visitors. Come across the moat."

Delvar raised an eyebrow. "A moat? I thought it was a lake."

Majora walked over to the water's edge, stepping into her canoe. "Of course. Every castle worth its salt has a moat. Come on. The water isn't deep."

Obi tried to hide his embarrassment by looking away. He turned to Layna. "That boat was just across the lake, wasn't it?"

Layna nodded. "I don't know how she did that. I saw no rope or string."

"Layna, ask her how she did it."

Layna shook her head. "No, Obi. That would be impolite. No user of magic likes to tell their secrets."

Majora picked up a short pole, using it to push the small craft across the lake. "Come on! Don't be shy. I use the canoe, because I don't like getting my feet wet."

The party hesitated at the water's edge. Vestos looked at Obi, giving him a nod. Obi could tell Vestos was waiting for Obi to see how deep the water was. Raising his robes to his waist, he took a step into the murky water. The moat bottom was boggy and difficult to walk across. He felt uncertain in the way his footing shifted as he walked. He carefully made his way onto the island. The others waited until he was safely across before they crossed the moat. He wondered if they were waiting to see if he would be eaten by an alligator.

Majora's Island was dry, hard-packed land with sparse grass. Spaced evenly around the island's perimeter stood small stakes. Layna bent close to the first one. "These sticks are curious. What do you think they mean?"

The short stakes made Obi uneasy. He had seen similar totems in the monastery's library books, but he had always imagined them much taller. He bent close to one with a small white skull. It had shiny rocks for eyes and small thin bones lining the stake. "I think these are wards for the illiterate."

Layna traced a finger along a skull and wrinkled her nose at him.

Obi could tell that she didn't believe him. He explained, "You know, they serve as a warning for people who can't read."

Layna went around, peering at each totem, studying it before moving on to the next. She stopped at one with a large skull and poked her finger at it. "Awfully short for people. Perhaps these are a warning for rats not to enter the island." She called out, "Majora, what are these totems for?"

Majora stood at the front door of her house and called back, "You can cook your rabbits at the fire but don't touch the pig."

Layna stood tall, cocking her head sharply. "She was just at the moat. How did she make it to her house so quickly?"

Obi could see Layna had questions, and so did he. It was strange that Majora would live in the middle of a swamp and even stranger that her canoe had crossed the moat by itself. Obi had so many questions with so few answers.

Layna gently felt along the edge of a skull, examining its large fangs. The skull was larger than the rest, about the size of her fist. "This looks like a large rat. No, on second thought, it is a weasel."

Tannon shouted, "Layna, stop! Leave that alone. You don't know where it has been."

She stuck out her tongue at him. Not waiting for his response, she ran down to the fire pit. Tannon bolted after her.

Obi followed them to the roasting pig. The pig had turned a light brown color with darker strips. Clear juices streaked down the skin, then into the hot coals, making a sizzling sound. It reminded Obi of the monastery, when the senior brothers would roast a pig for the harvest moon festival. They would always make it smell so good. He took in a deep breath; the savory aromas made his mouth water and stomach growl.

Layna stood next to the fire. She drew out three rabbits from her pack, field-dressed and ready to roast.

Obi had seen only one rabbit drop from the sky right onto Tark's chest. He had laughed so hard his cheeks were still sore. "When did these rabbits drop from the sky?"

She looked up at him and gave him a mischievous little smile. He knew that she was not going to tell him. He asked again. She ignored him. She placed the rabbits next to the coals.

Tannon scratched his head. "No wonder you were all about giving back the silver, because you already had these rabbits before the first one dropped out of the sky."

She turned to Tannon with a fierceness in her eyes. "My business is my business, not yours, little brother. You're not Father. I don't have to answer to you."

"You're not Mother, but you act just like her."
"No I don't! You take that back!"

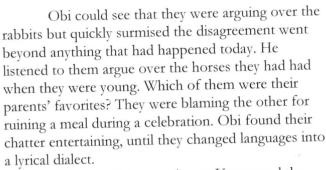

Obi could see that they were arguing over the rabbits but quickly surmised the disagreement went beyond anything that had happened today. He listened to them argue over the horses they had had when they were young. Which of them were their parents' favorites? They were blaming the other for ruining a meal during a celebration. Obi found their chatter entertaining, until they changed languages into a lyrical dialect.

Obi turned his attention to Vestos and the others. They had put their bedrolls in the barn, and everyone looked famished. Vestos held his pot, filled with soaking grains for tomorrow's breakfast. "Ah, siblings. They always fight. My brother and I used to get into some real throw downs. You surprise me, Obi. You don't miss much, do you? You are not the common monk, with a nose constantly in a book or copying scripts."

Obi didn't know what to say; he was just like any other monk. He tried hard to listen and be part of the team. He shrugged. "That pig looks close to being done."

Vestos said, "As Tug would say, that pig is good enough to eat. On the bright side, we will be having roasted rabbit after all."

Majora appeared at their side. "I have some homemade stew that will go well with your rabbits."

Vestos and Obi jumped. "Where did you come from?"

Majora giggled. "You men are jumpy."

Vestos squinted at her for a moment, as if he were trying to see something more, to see something unseen.

She squinted back. "Vestos, do you have something in your eye?"

Surprised, he stiffened up. "Ah, oh, … no."

She pointed to Tug and Obi. "If I could impose, could you two take that pig down to the docks and put it on the mount? Just don't touch it, whatever you do."

Obi was glad to lend a hand but wanted to ask why he couldn't touch it.

Majora looked at him, with the same look Obi had received from Layna, when he had asked her about the rabbits. Majora wasn't going to answer him either, even if he asked.

Obi and Tug picked up the pig by the spit and hauled it down to the dock. Exactly like Majora had said, at the end of the pier sat two small iron Y-shaped pieces. They hauled the pig across the dock and placed it in the mounts. Obi scratched his head. "Why is she putting it down here? It isn't like we would steal her pig."

Tug looked at the roasted pig, making a smacking sound.

Obi backed away. "You heard Majora, and you shouldn't mess with that pig."

Tug scoffed and pinched off a large piece of shoulder meat. He blew on it before putting it in his mouth.

Obi shook his head and was tempted to waggle a finger at him but didn't. Tug had an edge to his attitude, which Obi didn't want to trifle with. He turned and ran back to the fire pit.

Tannon and Layna had stopped arguing and were making faces at each other. Tark had taken off his armor and had replaced it with a red shirt and tan breeches. Delvar was still in his armor, except for his cloak—no doubt hung up to dry.

In a short time the aroma of roasted rabbit filled the air. Layna pulled them off the fire and began cutting up the meat into bite-size portions.

Majora came out with a large black pot of soup with onions, spiced with red peppers, and placed it on the hook and swung it over the fire.

Layna took a deep breath. "Is that garlic soup?"

Majora brightened. "Yes, it is. This soup will put some hair on your chest. Have you had garlic soup before?"

"Our mother use to make that for us on special occasions. It even has toasted bread crumbs on top of it. May I taste it?"

Majora waved her and Tannon in, closer to the soup. "Of course you can. Have as much as you like."

Layna picked up a ladle and put a helping of garlic soup in her bowl and placed the meat on top.

Tark noticed the rabbits, and promptly gave Layna two silver coins and handed out the other silver pieces to their party. He rubbed his hands together and gave his compliments for the dinner.

The roasted rabbit tasted of Vestos's spices, the soup hot and hearty with small crunchy portions of onions and toasted bread. Obi found the spices in the soup made his eyes water and heated him up from the inside out.

By the time everyone ate their fill, long shadows stretched across the island. The party members had moved their packs into the barn, while Obi was happy to tend the fire. Majora offered more soup before taking her pot back into her house, returning with small sweet cakes. They were the size of his palm, sprinkled with roasted nuts and raisins with honey drizzled over the top. Obi wanted to save half of his portion for his morning breakfast, but, it was so good, he just had to finish it, and he did.

Delvar gave a well-rehearsed courtly bow. "Thank you, Majora. You are an exceptional host and a fine cook."

She gave him a little smile. "Oh, I like visitors. No one ever visits me in the swamp."

Delvar, fidgeting with his mustache, said, "When we were almost here, we heard a wicked growling howl. I don't know what made it."

Majora's eyes widened; a mischievous smile crossed her face. "A growl, you say, and a howl too?"

He nodded. "Yes, that's right, just before we got here."

She took a deep breath and brought her hands to her mouth, letting out a low rumbling growl that transformed into a mournful howl.

Obi had heard dogs, wolves, and screeching birds howl but never anything close to that sound. He looked at Tark and Delvar, who looked pale and unsettled.

Delvar stuttered, "Yes, that's it. That is the howl I heard. Was that you out there?"

Majora gave him a wicked, toothy grin. "No, I heard it too. That sound is the call of the swamp people."

Obi raised his hand. "Swamp people? You mean, more people live out here?"

Her eyes gleaming in the final rays of sunlight, she said, "All sort of things live here in the swamp. I am surprised that you men didn't come face-to-face with some of the locals."

Obi hadn't seen any signs of anyone living in the swamp, but that didn't interest him. He wanted to know about the totems, the boat, and more. He blurted out, "Why do you have the pig at the dock?"

Majora looked up at the sun and back to the party. "I was wondering which of you would ask me about that. That pig is for the swamp people. It is an offering to them to keep the peace. Think of it as a goodwill gesture."

Obi thought that made good sense, to keep in the good graces with friends in a swamp. It was the same with the monastery, but it wasn't done for a roasted pig, but for wine, labor, and letter-writing.

Majora turned to Delvar. "What brings you to my doorstep?"

Delvar began slowly. "We are going to Midreach, as we said. But we heard this story from a bard a while back about dragons and a terrible war and a great wall. We want to see these things for ourselves. Have you heard of these stories?"

Majora cackled. "My, my, you are young and brave to seek out a beast like a dragon."

"You have heard of them?" Delvar asked.

She warned, "Yes, I know of the Dragonwall and its terrible history. It is no mere story, and dragons are no myth. You would be well served to leave all things dragon alone. There is no force of nature more destructive or dangerous than a dragon."

Obi said, "Surely dragons are gone from the world. I mean, no one has ever seen one!"

Majora corrected, "No one LIVING. The dead only rarely tell tales, and rarer still are their tales happy."

Delvar insisted, "I have heard something of dragon treasure. If the dragons are gone, then maybe there is fortune to be had north of this Dragonwall."

Majora shook her head. "I will not waste my breath arguing that but ask you this. How many men have you encountered who have dragon treasure, and how many only have stories?"

Obi spoke up. "I only wish to see the wall and perhaps a dragon. I do not wish for treasure beyond this."

Majora pointed her finger at Obi and gave him a knowing smile. "Knowledge is its own treasure. That's true. But what you seek maybe the last thing you learn."

Obi rose up. "Seeing a dragon would be wonderful!"

Majora attested, "A dragon is a sight, I am sure, child, but make sure you are not seen. You and your friends would hardly be a snack. A dragon will end you with no more thought than you stepping on an ant."

"So it is true? What we heard of the war, and why the wall was built?" Delvar asked.

She shook her head. "Well, I do not know what you were told, but, yes, centuries ago there was a terrific struggle between men and their allies against the dragon kind. Many terrible battles were fought, most of them north of the Dragonwall."

"Just to be clear, the dragons are not far from the wall?" Obi asked.

"Farther than you know. The lands on which those battles were fought are not claimed by man or dragon. They are haunted by the restless spirits that died in the fighting. It's said that they come out at night and stalk the land under moonless skies. Any that fall into their clutches are damned for all eternity."

Obi did not like the sound of being damned for eternity. He didn't like the idea of restless spirits; he gulped. "We didn't hear anything like that."

Majora stood up. "Well, old Majora tells you now. Do not find yourself north of the Dragonwall at night. You will surely regret it. Come. It is getting late. The swamp people do not like strangers, and I don't want any misunderstandings with them. All of you listen to me. Go into the barn, and do not come out till it is daylight. I will come and get you."

Obi could see many of their party didn't like being told what to do. Tug looked irritated, and so did Tannon. Obi didn't mind sleeping in a barn, but he had hoped to see the swamp people.

Tark clapped his hands together. "Majora, thank you for your hospitality and goodwill, and we will gladly respect your wishes and stay in the barn."

Obi raised his hand. "What do the swamp people look like?"

Tark gave him a dark look, which made Obi put his hand down.

With a feeble-looking hand, Majora patted Tark across his thick arms. "The swamp people are not really people at all. They are smart animals, nothing more. If they smell you, they might decide to eat you. That's why I didn't want you to touch the pig. That smell drives them wild."

Tug's ears perked up. He smelled his hands and jacket.

Obi's eyes went wide, while he sniffed at Tug and scooted away from him. "Really, beasts? And they are attracted to roasted pig?"

Majora threw her head back, letting out a wild cackling laugh. "No, but I had you going."

Tug and Obi let out a nervous laugh, as the others laughed loudly.

Majora wiped a tear from her eye. "The swamp people are a little odd-looking but just people. They are skittish about strangers. They probably wouldn't like it, if they knew I had guests. It would put me in an awkward spot. Just stay in the barn until morning, and everything will be all right."

Obi reluctantly nodded, heading to the barn. "I wanted to see the swamp people."

Tark clapped again, getting everyone's attention. "To the barn."

The barn was dark and warm. It felt good to be dry for a change. Obi listened for any sounds outside. At first he could only hear the others breathing, then a light scratching sound.

The barn door swung open. Obi jumped and screamed.

Majora walked in with a glowing lantern. "Thought you might want to see a little before going to bed."

Obi tried to contain his surprise.

She gave a smile and a giggle. "Did you think I was a swamp person?"

Delvar rolled up on his elbow. "I will protect you, Obi!"

Laughter erupted from the party, as Majora let out another loud cackle. She moved to the center of the barn, where a thick chain hung down from the rafters. She secured the lantern on the hook. "Don't worry about the lantern. Just let it burn, and don't worry about the swamp people. You leave them alone, they will leave you alone. You men and lady get some rest. I will make you a hearty breakfast in the morning."

Obi watched Majora give them a final look and then leave, closing the barn doors behind her. He listened to her footfalls heading toward the house.

Everyone unfolded their bedrolls and stretched out on the straw. Obi climbed to the loft, hoping to find a window or an exit where he could peek out. He found none. "How can I see the swamp people, if I don't have a window?"

Tark shot him a look. Obi could make out his disapproval. Obi moved back down the ladder and to the door. He checked his pack and writing book.

Vestos stretched, pushing straw out of his way. He rolled up on an elbow. "Delvar, what are you doing, sleeping in your armor?"

Delvar fluffed a heap of straw around his pack, making a pillow. "Don't you worry about how I sleep. Between you and me, I don't like the idea of the swamp people creeping around outside, while we hide like children."

Vestos arched an eyebrow. "We are staying in the barn as a favor to our host. Majora didn't have to let us stay here. In fact she could have insisted that we move on."

Delvar said, "Majora gives me the creeps. She moves like the wind, when we turn away, and appears when she isn't called. There is more to this woman than meets the eye."

Vestos yawned. "She is a spry old woman. There are some things that bother me about our host."

Delvar bit his lip. "No, I don't buy it, not one little bit, and she is lying to us. We might wake up hip deep in swamp people. Only I will be safe, sleeping in my armor."

Vestos waggled a finger at him. "Is that why you're still in your armor? More important, did you notice how large that roasted pig was, and how small she is? That pig looked twice her size. How did she kill it? How did she get it on the spit? I tried to see beyond her appearance but couldn't."

Obi did notice that the pig was easily twice her size. She was thin and frail-looking with many secrets. "Those curious little poles with skulls are very unusual, and she lives alone in the swamp. It is all very eccentric."

Tug and Tark discussed unusual things they had noticed, like who helped her build this house using timbers so large it would take ten men to move them. They talked about how many people it would take to haul the wood through the swamp to build the buildings.

Obi listened to all the questions about Majora, and each person made good points. She did move fast, and her boat had crossed the moat by itself. The totems were a little unusual, but nothing she had done had been really overtly menacing, except her humor and the way she ogled him. Obi knew that Majora had secrets. Vestos had realized it when they had first arrived, but Obi didn't care about that. Everyone has secrets. He wanted to see the swamp people. They were much more interesting to him than who built the house.

Obi sat back, trying to imagine what the swamp people might look like, while he listened for any sound outside the barn. He pictured them tall like elves or short as dwarves. Were they covered in mud, like the drawing in some of the books he had read in the monastery library? "I have heard of really short people who throw spears. Perhaps that is why Majora has those totems."

Vestos disagreed. "I have never heard of such things."

Obi made a face. "Well, I am just anxious to see the swamp people. Come on, I won't talk or be seen by them. I just want to see them, so I can draw a picture and add it to the book."

Tark had had enough of the chatter. He cleared his throat. "No, we made a deal. We won't go out until morning."

Obi plopped down in the straw next to the door and listened to all the idle chatter, till it died down. He wanted to tell Tark that Obi had made no such deal, but a stern look from Tark made Obi keep quiet.

Tark used his scale shirt as a makeshift pillow and was fast asleep. Tannon lay in the far corner, already fluffing straw in an area, making a barrier around his sister, while Vestos yawned loudly and rolled to his side. Tug and Delvar stretched out, taking up most of the floor space.

It seemed like only a short time had passed when everyone in the barn had been claimed by sleep, marked by light snoring. Everyone had a light snore, except Vestos, who had a raspy snort, until he rolled to his side. Obi soon found himself the only one awake.

Obi wrestled with his curiosity, trying to think of a way to see the swamp people. Majora had been very clear about staying inside the barn but so was the promise he had made to his Sovereign. He tried to think of a solution to satisfy the promise to his Sovereign and to Majora, then it occurred to him; he didn't have to leave the barn. He could take a small peek outside, and everyone would be satisfied. Obi made up his mind. He would not endanger his companions by leaving the barn, and he could honor the Sovereign by looking outside to see something of interest.

Obi carefully and quietly got up from his bedroll and crept over to the barn door. The lantern Majora had provided was turned low but still easily illuminated the interior of the small barn. The building had a warm, cozy, safe feeling but not what he would expect of a shelter for farm animals. He glanced back; his friends were asleep.

A lingering thought had bothered him since they had arrived on the island. Majora had a barn, but where were the animals? Doubt crept forward from the back of his mind. There was so much about Majora that did not make sense. Perhaps he should just return to bed and forget the swamp people.

Obi paused, turning back to the door. He had to know, and he had to see. He peeked out a small crack where two boards met in the door but soon realized he would have to open the door, if he was going to see anything at all. He paused again, chewing his lower lip.

If he were alone, this would be easy. It was a risk he was willing to take. However, if there was a problem, he would be endangering everyone. Obi struggled with his obligation to the Sovereign, his friends, and his own curiosity. He promised himself, if there were any danger, he would close the door, and no harm would be done.

Six

Not what you say but how you say it.

Summoning his courage, Obi put his hands on the door to push it open. The door moved just a few inches. He heard something. A faint stealthy footstep with a light floral scent made him pause at the door. He recognized it immediately, the scent of roses. His heart skipped a beat.

"Obi, be very quiet." Majora's soft voice seemed to be right in his ear.

Obi stifled a scream, yet a warm feeling washed over him. Instead of jumping out of his skin, like a child with his hand caught in a pie, he calmly waited for Majora to open the door, as if he had been expecting her.

"I thought as much," Majora commented softly. "The mark of curiosity was too bold on your face to expect you to not try and see the swamp people."

Obi stared at his toes, then grinned slightly, and looked Majora in the eye. "I have to know. I have to see."

Majora held a finger to her lips. From the folds in her robe she withdrew a leather necklace, decorated with small bone beads and a sharp claw the size of Obi's thumb. Majora slipped the necklace over Obi's head. "This talisman will show the swamp people that you are under my protection."

Obi had so many questions but kept quiet.

Majora looked knowingly at Obi's waist. "I got to see fine things, and so you should get to see something too."

Obi wondered which was more dangerous, the swamp people or Majora. How she had ogled him when he had dressed, and how she had teased him about staying in the house with her, saying something about spoiling him for any other woman. He had no doubt she could have made good on that boast. He felt his ears turning red again.

She patted him on the cheek and took him by the hand. "To see a thing for a thing is an even trade. Now be quiet, and don't make any sudden moves. The swamp people are nervous and quick to anger."

Majora opened the barn door and looked out. She smiled at Obi, still holding his hand, and with the other beckoned him to come outside.

Obi was excited and more than a little nervous. Doubt made his stomach knot with the nagging notion that maybe this wasn't a good idea. He reassured himself; surely if Majora had meant him harm, there were other ways that were less risky to her. Obi carefully stepped through the door and quietly closed it behind him. It was very dark out; the moon was hidden behind a spotty layer of clouds. Obi blinked hard, trying to get his eyes to adjust from the barn's brighter interior to this dim starlight.

Obi leaned over to ask Majora a question, but she cut him off with her fingers to her lips and a slight shake of her head. She pointed out toward the dock, where he and Tug had taken the pig. Obi could see some movement in the water but could not make out what the thing was. He watched intently. He caught his breath when the clouds moved away from the moon.

In the soft moonlight, a large muscular figure climbed from the water onto the dock. Silent as smoke and pale as the moon that revealed its form, it was manlike but clearly not a man. It stood upright—tall, naked, and heavily muscled—and moved with a balanced grace. Its feet were large and ended in black claws. It had powerful oversize hands that had large black curved nails.

Although the beast looked human, Obi could make out its face. That sent a chill across him, making him almost paralyzed with terror. He might have run, but Majora had a firm grip on his hand. Her presence seemed to decrease his feeling of dread. Almost as quickly as it came, it faded.

Obi wanted to look away but stared directly at the swamp man's wide mouth that reminded him of a frog. In the moonlight, he could make out the long white pointed fangs that jetted from the corners. Its large eyes were wide set, and, when it turned its head just right, they would glow with a fierce yellow light.

The hair on its head was as black as its nails and stood straight up, like a crest on the ridge of its skull. Obi knew he should be terrified, but he was calm, like he was watching from some safe place, where he could not be reached by those vicious fangs and horrible claws. The creature was joined by several more just like the first. They were cautious, smelling the air and looking around. Each paused a moment when they scanned Majora and Obi, but none made a move toward them.

Once assured we were no threat, the swamp people attacked the roast boar. Obi was mesmerized by their brutal feeding, watching them making their low growling noises while tearing large mouthfuls of flesh and crunching bone.

He watched till the pig was half gone. Majora pushed him back into the barn. "The lowland friends are not likely to bother you when they finish the pig, but why take the chance? Now you go to sleep, and we will talk again in the morning."

Majora closed the barn door when she left. Obi found himself in his blankets without really knowing how he got there. He knew he should be as excited as he had ever been, but instead he lay down and closed his eyes and was soon in a dreamless sleep.

Obi awoke early in the morning, disturbed and excited by the night's events. It seemed more like a dream than being real; besides, no one had seen the swamp people except Majora and him. He pulled out the writing book that the Sovereign had given him, along with several pieces of charcoal, and began sketching what he had seen. He made an outline, and he glanced down at the necklace with the large claw dangling down, the one Majora had given him. He grabbed it tightly. "This was proof that last night was real," he said to himself and, with renewed vigor, sketched out the rest of the swamp people. He made sure to capture the large mouth, hands, and big feet of the first one he had seen. He created a good representation, including their ridge of hair and large muscles and fangs. Once satisfied, he wrapped up the book and put it back into his pack.

The rest of the party still slept. He rolled out of bed and headed to the fire pit. Most of the embers were cold, but he found a few hot coals in the center. He added wood and quickly had a fire. He returned to the barn, rolled up his bedroll and pillow, then secured it to his small pack. He checked his crossbow and counted his bolts. He had six days of rations and water, and a few silver pieces. He checked the writing book and couldn't wait to show the rest of his party what they had missed.

Vestos was the next to rise from the barn, then Tark, Layna, and her brother, Tannon. Each looked refreshed. When everyone was awake, Obi pulled out his writing book to show them his drawing. Each member had been initially excited to see the drawing, then silence enveloped the party. Even Delvar's smile faded to a look of concern. Obi began to feel a little out of place; perhaps he shouldn't have shown them the picture, or perhaps he shouldn't have peeked at the swamp people. He felt uneasy.

Tark stared at the drawing, as if to memorize it. "After I told you to stay inside the barn, you went outside and saw this thing last night?"

Obi nodded. "Majora came for me last night and opened the door."

Tug gave him a grin. "Told you that she had a crush on you."

Obi thought that too but ignored him. "I was just going to peek at the swamp people. A small peek, then I would close the door."

Tark's expression darkened. "You exposed us. You exposed the sleeping party to these creatures. How many were there?"

Obi took a half step back. "Six maybe. It was difficult to see them, and they moved silently."

Tark took the writing book, examined the drawing. "And this here, what is in their hands?"

Obi took another step back. He could feel the anger brewing inside Tark. Obi didn't intend to make anyone mad. He cleared his throat. "Those were claws, black sharp claws."

The knot he had felt last night returned, threatening to double him over. Obi felt stunned by the revelation. He had thought it was an acceptable risk just to peek outside, but Tark was right. If it had gone wrong, the whole party would have been in danger. The whole party could have been killed. "I am sorry. I didn't intend for anything to go wrong."

Tark's light blue eyes darkened. He flipped through the pages of the writing book and back to the drawing. "Damn it, Obi, of all the stupid things to do!"

Obi bit his lip. "I am sorry, Tark. I wasn't thinking."

"Damn right you were not thinking! Hell, I have a good mind to give you a thrashing right here, just so you will never forget!"

Obi could feel his face and ears flush. He wanted to run away, but, if the Sovereign would hear of Obi's cowardice, his master surely would be disappointed in Obi. He might be beaten for doing such a brazen act without a thought to the rest of the party. His shoulders sank, and he bowed his head, and, in a voice just above a whisper, he said, "If that is what you think is best, so be it."

Tark took a long hard look into Obi's eyes.

Obi could feel Tark's stare and didn't know where to look. He didn't want to stare at Tark; that would surely make him angrier. But if Obi continued to look down, Tark might think it disrespectful. Obi stared straight ahead.

Tark got nose to nose with Obi, for what felt like an hour. Making a pinched look, Tark's tone softened. "No, I don't think that would help. Just don't do it again."

Obi shook his head vigorously. "I swear, Tark! I won't ever put the party at risk."

Tark took the book into his hands, staring at the drawing. "How big are these things?"

Obi raised his arm over his head. "Big and broad."

Tark gave the book back to Obi, swinging a wide turn. "I am getting my gear from the barn, and I suggest the rest of you do the same."

Tug peeked at the drawing. "What the hell? I thought Majora said they were people."

"I think she said that so not to frighten us," Vestos said in a soft voice.

Tug growled. "I liked the swamp a whole lot more yesterday, when we only had to worry about flying rabbits. Now freaky swamp people. I don't like this place one little bit. I can tell you that for nothing."

Everyone nodded.

Tark's mood darkened. "I want to see Majora. I need to talk with her."

Obi shook his head. "No, Tark. Do not be mad at her. She did nothing but assist me to see the swamp people. The fault lies with me alone."

Tark made a fist with his right hand, studying Obi's eyes, staring at him as if waiting for him to back down.

Obi didn't move. The senior brothers at the monastery would do the same thing to him. At first he would wince or flinch, and they would punch him. Each time the hits would be harder than the time before, until he had had enough and decided to stand up to the elder monks. After a few fistfights, they stopped trying to stare him down. Although Tark's gaze was fierce and his blue eyes seemingly stared directly into his soul, Obi was not going to flinch.

Tark took a deep breath. "You're right, Obi. She didn't do anything wrong. But that isn't what I wanted to talk to her about. I was hoping that she knew the shortest way to the Dragonwall."

In raspy voice Majora spoke. "Of course I do, and I will point you in the right direction."

Both Obi and Tark jumped. Vestos gave a small chuckle. "Good morning, Majora. Obi was telling us of the swamp people and showing us the picture he drew."

She set a large pot next to the fire. "This will be done soon. I would like to see that picture too."

Obi opened the book to the drawing of the swamp people.

She turned a sharp eye at the picture. She looked it over and threw her head back, letting out a loud cackle. "My boy, you do have a gift for drawing! That really captures the essence of the swamp people. You even got their hair ridge and claws. You were paying attention."

Obi nodded slightly. "Thank you."

Delvar pointed at the picture. "That is what the swamp people look like?"

She gave him a crooked grin. "Yes, that's right. Obi did a good job drawing them, although I would have given that one a larger manhood. He was quite well endowed."

Layna waved her hand. "I would like to see that picture again. I didn't see it clearly before."

Tannon rolled his eyes. Obi handed her the drawing. She looked at it carefully, cocking her head to one side, then to the other, before addressing Majora, crinkling her nose. "It is larger than that?"

She grinned and held up her arm pointing to her elbow. "Yes, much larger."

Layna squealed, and they both giggled.

Tug peeked at the drawing. "Yes, almost as big as mine."

The guys broke into a nervous laugh, except for Tark, who went to the barn, retrieving his gear.

The kettle lid rattled, signaling it was ready. Obi began scooping out large spoonfuls of gruel onto the awaiting plates. "Breakfast!"

Vestos smacked his lips. "I taste honey and grains and a few herbs I am not familiar with. Damn, Majora, yours is much better than mine!"

Majora, apparently pleased, said, "I can show you the herbs, if you like, and the special ones that give it the earthy aroma."

Vestos smiled from ear to ear., "Yes, that would be very kind. How can I repay you for your hospitality?"

Majora waved him off. "You might be hard-pressed to find some of these herbs outside of the swamp, but you can dry them, and they will keep for a long time without losing their flavor."

Vestos had a second bowl. "You are an amazing woman, Majora, and more versatile than all of us combined."

She patted his cheek. "I am probably older than all of you combined too." She laughed loudly at her own joke.

Tark brought his pack, setting it beside the fire ring, and helped himself to a bowl of porridge.

Majora's smile faded slightly, and her expression turned more serious. "You are going over the Dragonwall to see a dragon? Yes?"

Tark nodded.

She continued. "I doubt if I could make it there and back myself. Since you're going over there anyway, could you retrieve an item for me?"

Tark's mood lightened. "What is it?"

She held up her hands about a foot apart. "A box, about this big. It would mean a lot to me."

Obi nodded in agreement. "That shouldn't be a problem. We are going over there anyway to look for dragons."

Tark shot him a look.

Obi cursed himself for blurting this out, as if speaking for them all, and bit his lip. "Well, that is, if the rest of the party agrees."

Tug snickered and said, in a low voice just so Obi could hear, "Obi has a girlfriend, a little old for you, but what the hell. She will curl your toes."

Obi fell silent.

Tark looked sideways at him, then back to Majora. "I think we can handle bringing back a box."

"Before you agree, I must warn you," she cautioned. "The spot you're going across is quite dangerous, but I guess you're prepared for danger."

Tug thumped his chest, making a loud noise. Delvar did the same. They gave a nod to Tark.

Tark rubbed his chin whiskers. "We will be happy to bring back the box."

Majora continued to stir the porridge. "Once you're over the wall, travel only during the day. If you're caught over there during the night, hide and wait till morning. All manner of bad things come out at night."

Obi perked up. "What kind of bad things?"

Tug slapped his thick sword. "Nothing that cold steel can't kill or dismember."

Majora raised a crooked finger toward Obi and Tug. "I hear the undead roam at night and other real bad things. I don't want your deaths on my conscious."

A chill went through Obi, making his eyes grow wide. It was bad enough to worry about alligators and snakes but the undead? That was terrifying. Tark, Delvar, and Tug seemed unmoved by the mention of the undead, but the word made Obi's heart beat fast. "Really, undead? How do you kill something that is already dead?"

Tark smirked. "Okay, where do we find this box?"

Majora tapped her long bony finger alongside her cheek. "Straight over the wall past the river about a half day's journey, there is a town with a church still standing. Under the church's pedestal lays an ornately carved box. You will know it when you see it."

"That's it?"

She nodded. "Anything of riches is yours for the taking. I just want the box."

Tug leaned forward. "What is this about treasure and gold?"

She cleared her throat. "At one time that town was a very wealthy town, but that was some years ago."

Tug pushed in a bit more. "Count me in."

Everyone agreed.

Tark clapped his hands together. "Done. We will go retrieve your box and bring it back."

Her mischievous grin broadened to a full smile. "I was hoping you were going to accept my offer, so I have something for all of you. It is a special charm, just like the one Obi is wearing."

Tark walked right up to Obi and took a hold of the necklace that Majora had given him. "This is new. Did you make it? What kind of claw is this?"

Majora reached into the fold of her garment, withdrawing six similar leather necklaces decorated with small bone beads and a sharp claw the size of Obi's thumb. "These necklaces will serve as a badge while you're in the swamp. Everyone who knows me will recognize the necklace and will not harm you. It is a symbol that you are under my protection."

Making a face like he smelled something sour, Tug asked, "Does that go for the swamp people too?"

Her smiled dimmed, replaced with a cautious look. She pointed to a hornet's nest on the side of the barn. "Have you heard the term, don't poke the beehive?"

Tug shook his head.

She leaned in close to him, looking into his eyes, then into Tark's. "While you're in the swamp, don't go looking for trouble. You don't mess with them, and they will not mess with you. Got it?"

Tark shot Tug a pinched look. "We got it. Let's pack up and get moving. We will see you in a few days, if everything goes right."

Majora cautioned, "Remember. If you're over the wall during the nighttime, hide, stay quiet, and wait till morning."

Tark nodded, as did several others. Majora pulled Delvar and Layna to the side, giving them instructions to the Dragonwall. Once she was sure that they had the directions down, she gave them a wave and retreated into her home.

Tark pointed to Delvar and Layna. They turned and headed off the island, slogging through the shallowest part of the moat; the rest of the party followed.

Ever since Tark had seen the picture of the swamp people, his mood had seemed to worsen. Obi began to realize what Tark had already concluded. The thought make his palms sweat. Yesterday all they had to worry about was catching falling rabbits and keeping their feet dry. Since last night, everything had changed. If creatures like the swamp people existed, then, perhaps, creatures like dragons existed too. Obi wondered if all the dragon stories might be true. Silently Obi wished he were back at the monastery.

Seven

A quest for a box.

Obi splashed across the pond Majora called her moat. On the far side he turned and waved a final good-bye to the old woman. Majora waved back enthusiastically. "Write down all your adventures, sweet buns. I will want to hear every detail."

Obi smiled and turned away.

Vestos eyed Obi with mock seriousness. "I do believe she wants to marry you."

"I don't think so."

Vestos laughed and slapped Obi on the back. "Cheer up. There will be other women!"

Trying to change the subject, Obi muttered, "We had better catch up with the others."

Vestos laughed again.

They walked through the morning; the ground became drier and firmer. The tall swamp grass gave way to shorter field grass, and it became clear that they were climbing out of the valley.

Running to catch up with the party, Tannon said, "It seems we are making incredible time, compared to making our way here."

Vestos gave Tannon a smile. "Yes, we were discussing that very thing. Tark is convinced it is because we had a good night's rest. I say the terrain is drier here than coming down the valley."

Tannon shook his head. "You're both wrong. I think it is the necklace Majora gave us. We are not fighting with the swamp. The swamp is simply letting us pass."

Vestos raised an eyebrow, considering the idea. "We could perform an experiment. You could take off your necklace, and I could carry it and see if you receive a snake bite, or fall into a bog or something."

Tannon shook his head. "No! It was my idea. How about you take off your necklace and give it to me, and we will see what happens to you?"

Vestos declined. "Whatever the reason, we are making good time."

The firm ground rose. Field flowers bloomed, and bushes and trees grew tall—the same type of trees that Obi and Tug had gathered walking sticks from, when they had first entered the swamp. At a small patch of purple flowers Vestos bent to take a closer look. He pulled a few of the leaves and tasted them. He called to Obi, "I will only be a moment."

Curious at what he had stopped to examine, Obi waited for him.

Vestos quickly stuffed his pockets full of the dark green leaves and purple flowers, and then hurried to catch up with Obi.

Obi asked, "Vestos, what do you have there?"

"Some of the herbs that made Majora's grain so tasty. I don't recall the name she called it, but I tasted it, and it is the same one. It will last for a long time, if dried."

Tug walked up behind them and withdrew a piece of wood about an arm's length long. "She showed me how to sharpen my blade to a razor edge with this stick. Damnedest thing I ever seen, but it works like a charm. My blade is sharp enough you can shave with it."

Tannon laughed. "She showed me how I can make a snare, using a piece of leather and a stick, and to catch fish with the same snare. What did she teach you, Obi?"

Obi bit his lip. "We traded tasks. I showed her how to bind pages into a book, and she showed me how to track a person using two sticks."

Vestos grinned. "That is amazing! Majora is a spry old woman."

Obi shook his head in disbelief. "Majora is quite versatile in her hidden talents. Did she teach everyone something during our short stay?"

Tannon scratched his head, then stopped, putting a finger to his temple. "I think so. She was showing Layna some plant that stops bleeding, and, if chewed and placed on a snake bite, it will slow the poison."

Tark joined the men as they looked at the plants that Vestos had gathered. "What is wrong? Why have you stopped?"

"Vestos wanted to gather some herbs that Majora showed him how to use," Obi explained. "It seems Majora found time to teach each of us something useful. Did she show you anything?"

Tark pulled a piece of willow branch from his pocket. "If brewed into a tea, it will take away headaches and soothe sore muscles. How did Majora learn so many clever tricks?"

Looking at the branch, Tug laughed. "Majora got around to teaching all of us something. I saw her with Delvar, showing him how to get mud out of his cloaks."

Tark and Vestos gave him a big grin. Vestos let out a loud belly laugh. "That is so fitting for Delvar. Perhaps I have misjudged Majora. She seems a little eccentric, but I think she is a good person."

Obi thought so too. He couldn't help but wonder what Majora was like when she was younger. What sort of adventures would have led her to live in the swamp, make those short totems, and broker deals with creatures as dangerous as the swamp people? He wondered why she wanted a box from an abandon church. Could she be plotting something unpleasant? He tried to shrug off the idea and focused on the more important thing: seeing the Dragonwall.

By noon the temperature was climbing but not as high as during their time spent in the swamp. Obi's feet were tired, and his pace slowed, until he was last in line of the party. Up ahead Vestos and Tug were talking to Delvar, Tark, and Layna. They had stopped at the top of a small rise and were looking off to the north.

Obi hiked to the hilltop. "It is about time we took a break." He realized they had not stopped to rest but to examine the view. A quarter mile down the hill was a wall. The wall stretched as far as they could see to the east and to the west.

Vestos whistled. "It appears to be made of stone and quite wide. How tall do you think it is?"

Tug snorted. "Thirty feet tops. That lying bard said it was huge."

Vestos shook his head in disbelief. "Somehow I thought it would be much bigger and, you know, taller."

Tug agreed. "I know what you mean. It is impressively long, but it doesn't look like it would be much trouble for a dragon."

Vestos supposed, "Dragons can fly. So what's the use of a wall, especially one as low as that?"

Tug's mood soured. "I'm not impressed. We may as well take a rest, once we get to it."

A feeling of disappoint crossed over Obi. He thought the Dragonwall looked more like a raised road. They had traveled for such a long ways, and had heard the stories of how grand and spectacular the Dragonwall was supposed to be. Even Majora had said it was impressive. It was long, but the stories did them an injustice, coming to see a great wall, just to have it stand thirty feet high. Frustrated Obi took out his book and began sketching the wall, including the wide ramp and the gentle slope.

The party moved to the foot of a broad ramp. Several campsites and fire pits were scattered along the base of the wall; many looked recently used. They climbed the gentle slope; atop the wall, it was wide enough for two wagons to pass without trouble. Obi followed the group as they moved to look over the other side.

The party spoke no words, awestruck by the majestic view. Stretching out before them lay a broad and deep valley, full of dark green vegetation, colorful flowers, and tall trees. Hundreds of feet below, a wide and lazy river snaked its way east to west. The wall was made of stone and had been crafted by master engineers, who had used the shape of the hillside to their full advantage by following the highest and steepest points, as seen from the north side, which ensured the wall was completely unassailable.

Obi took out his book and began sketching. He soon had a rough image of the Dragonwall and could put in more details, once they camped. Amazement and awe overwhelmed him. Obi was the first to speak. "This certainly explains why we have heard so much of this famed Dragonwall. I would not believe such a thing existed, if we were not standing on it."

Delvar's tone had changed to astonishment. "Indeed, only a flying dragon could hope to breach such a fortification. The Dragonwall is magnificent, and purely an enormous undertaking to all who built it."

Obi stood beside Vestos. Far to the north Obi could see that the mountains rose once more and to a greater height, where the clouds roam. Closer he could see wide grassy fields dotted with groves of trees and shrubs. The land looked fertile and healthy. "This doesn't look like a battlefield."

Vestos nodded absently. "Obi, I was expecting a battle-hardened, desolate area, not rich fields. The land north of the Dragonwall looks like a particularly inviting area to live."

Obi scratched his head. Majora's stories conjured up a vile place of danger. Obi couldn't see any danger. "The trees are large and plentiful. The river looks to be calm and clean."

Vestos put a hand at his brow. "Look across the river. There are a score of deer grazing among the shrubs. This doesn't look to be the dangerous place that we have heard about."

Tannon said, "Yes, however, it is daytime. As I recall, everyone mentioned the dangers of being north of the Dragonwall after dark."

Looking into the valley, Obi picked up a stone and tossed it over the wall. He watched it fall, making distant clicking sounds. "That is what Majora said. It seems the farther we go toward the dragon lands, the less things are what they seem."

Waving a hand at the valley, Tug scoffed, "Bah! This wall may have had a purpose once. I bet the folks south have begun to believe their own stories too much. Do you see those deer? Deer do not graze peacefully, day or night, in a dangerous land."

Vestos stretched out his neck. "Can you see a town over there, across the river? I see something, but I can't really make it out."

Delvar placed a knee against the wall and struck a poise, pointing with his arm extended, using the other to catch the breeze in his cape. "I do see something. Looks like a valley goes down there. Difficult to tell from this distance."

Tark rolled his eyes at Delvar. "I have fifty feet of rope. Who else has some?"

Layna, Delvar, and Tug each pulled similar lengths from their packs. Tark began counting. "We have about two hundred feet of rope. That will get us down there easy enough."

Tannon gauged the sun's position. "I don't want to discount Majora's warning too quickly. It is getting late, and the sun will be setting."

Flashing his cloak out wide, Delvar put his hands in the sky, then to the horizon, before facing Tark. "I don't think we should risk getting over the wall today and not finding this place. We are running out of sunlight."

Tug took a drink from his water skin and gauged the sun for himself, mimicking Delvar's fancy hand movements.

Delvar didn't pay any attention to Tug's attempt to mock him. "Majora said it was past the river, about a half-day's walk to the church."

Seeing that his teasing didn't get any response, Tug let it go.

Tark clapped his hands together. "All right, let's camp here tonight, and, first thing in the morning, we cross—making sure we have enough time to make it to the church and back before sunset. If we have more time, we can do a little exploring while we are over there."

Everyone nodded in agreement and dropped their packs. Vestos pulled out his herbs he had found and set up his grains for the next day. Layna let Swiftwing take flight, in search of rabbits. Delvar sat on his pack, using the wall to lean against.

Obi looked down the low side of the wall. "Perhaps we should camp down there."

"Nah," Tug scoffed. "I want to see what moves around at night down in that valley. We should stay up here."

"I am curious myself," Tark commented.

Tug stood up from where he was rummaging in his pack and gave a low whistle. "We have company coming down the wall this way. It looks like a gaggle of men and horses. They have the stench of guards."

The party grabbed their gear and pulled it to one side, giving plenty of room for the coming horses. Even though the Dragonwall was wide enough so two wagons could pass one another, Obi could tell that Tark didn't want to give the soldiers any hint of trouble. Even from this distance Obi could see the first eight men were armored in polished chain mail. The weapons and armor of the approaching men caught the sunlight, making a spectacular display.

Tannon pointed out, "That shiny armor makes it difficult to see, but there are a dozen men marching behind them, wearing leather and carrying crossbows."

Vestos rolled his staff down his arm and leaned against the wall, making his appearance seem small and weak. Delvar stood tall, his cloak waving in the slight breeze, and stepped forward.

Under his breath, just so his voice wouldn't carry, Tug announced, "I bet that curly haired guy is going to stop and question us. He looks like trouble."

Tark shrugged. "In case anyone asks, we are going to Midreach. We are just travelers."

Vestos smiled at him with amusement dancing in his eyes. "They do have a sense of authority. Do you think Tug is right about them questioning us?"

A worried brow crinkled over his focused look, but Tark shook his head. "No, just being cautious."

The guard patrol plodded along the top of the wall, coming closer. It was soon apparent that the curly headed guard wore scale mail so polished that it outshone the others in chain mail.

Obi wondered how Tug had picked out the curly haired man as the leader from such a distance. Obi waited to see if Tug would be equally right about the curly haired man's disposition. Obi didn't have to wait long before the man in scale called to their party, "Hail, travelers."

Delvar flashed his cape and rolled a hand across his mustache. "Hail, good sir."

The curly haired guard sat stiffly upright on his horse, a flowing black cloak hung from his shoulders, secured to his armor. He spoke with a graveled voice. "I am Captain Samuel Jacobs of the Dragonwall Guard. You men can't camp here on the wall. It is forbidden."

Delvar gave a questioning look to Tark before answering, "Where would you like us to camp?"

He raised his hand for the rest of his men to halt before he dismounted. He stood nearly as tall as Vestos. The shiny scale armor and the black cloak had made him look much larger. Captain Jacobs's face darkened. "Clearly you men are not from around here. It is the law that travelers may use the road, but none other than the wall guard may camp on it. You may camp at the foot of the wall just there." He pointed down the ramp.

Delvar bowed slightly. "Of course we were unaware. We would be happy to camp below."

Captain Jacobs eyed them sternly. "What is your party doing on my wall?"

"We are merely traveling to Midreach," Delvar replied easily.

Captain Jacobs looked at them with a look of disdain. "Really? And what business do you have in Midreach?"

Obi heard Tug let out a low growl. He expected Tug to say something, say anything, but Tug kept quiet.

Delvar embellished, "Ah, well, the truth is, we are from the south, and we had heard stories of this great wall and wished to see it for ourselves. We felt that Midreach was the town closest to where we are now. We hope to find work there."

Captain Jacobs looked annoyed. "Well, I am sure honest men such as you will have no trouble finding work. Tell me, what is it you do?"

Obi began to get a little nervous. Captain Jacobs was clearly not very friendly. They had done nothing wrong, but the captain was doing a good job of making Obi feel otherwise.

Delvar replied smoothly, "My companions and I have many skills and are not shy to hard work."

The captain's expression turned dark; his eyes flared with danger. "Perhaps you are thinking to cross the wall and seek your fortune to the north?"

Delvar looked to valley below. "Oh, well, it does seem to have a lot to offer. My friends are fine hunters, and we noticed many deer just at the foot of the—"

Captain Jacobs cut him off, "Do you have a permit?"

"A permit? What the heck do I need a permit for?" Delvar snapped back.

Captain Jacobs explained, "The permit is to cross the Dragonwall."

Under his breath, but loud enough for Obi could hear, Tug grumbled, "What the hell? I told you this guy is a pain in the ass. Who needs a permit to scale a wall?"

If Delvar heard, he didn't let on. Delvar stifled a cough. "What did you say, Captain?"

Captain Jacobs looked annoyed. "As I was saying, the wall guard doesn't care if you cross the wall and head north. A word of caution though. Without a permit, we will not allow you to come back across the wall. The cold hard fact is, we will shoot anything attempting to scale and cross this wall."

Delvar turned to capture the wind in his cloak in a nonchalant yet purposeful movement. "Captain, we are simple men headed to Midreach. As you have pointed out, we are not from here. We have no intention of breaking any laws of this realm."

Obi was amazed by Delvar. If Obi hadn't known Delvar was lying, Obi would have believed his friend; also he could tell the captain did not believe anything they were saying. Obi wondered what was giving them away.

Captain Jacobs gave a smug look directed at Tark. "What is your name? Are you a dragon hunter? We don't want any dragon hunters, and no dragon magic should cross this wall either."

Tark chewed his lip a moment before answering, "My name is Tark, and I am definitely not a dragon hunter."

Taking Tark's lead, Delvar added, "No dragon hunters here, just travelers."

The captain snorted. "To obtain a permit to cross the wall, you will have to go to Midreach or Searreach. Midreach is quite a bit closer—about four days walking, two days by horse."

Delvar resumed his tale, how we were lost in the swamp and, with a little help from a hermit, had made it to the wall just recently.

Captain Jacobs ignored Delvar's story and went from person to person, looking them over, as if he were inspecting them.

Delvar continued telling his story of growing up in Delvingdeep and even included the bard's song that had started the journey.

The captain's mood changed slightly, from annoyed at repeating himself to more of an aloof behavior. He continued his well-rehearsed speech. "Gentlemen, since you say you're going to Midreach, life on the wall is dangerous. There are many things trying to cross the wall. Don't trust anything or anyone who doesn't have a permit."

Obi raised his hand. "What comes across the wall?"

Captain Jacobs stopped his pacing to stare at Obi. He had a dangerous look in his eye. "You will address me as Captain Jacobs or sir. Do you understand me?"

Obi felt small and wished he hadn't said anything to get his attention. "Yes, sir, Captain Jacobs."

Captain Jacobs resumed his pacing. "Excellent question. Bad things try to cross the wall. Dragon hunters mostly, trying to sneak back dragon magic or gold. Without a permit that is contraband. We get the occasional troll, goblin, and a smattering of undead types. But worst of all are fool-hearty adventurers who don't get a permit and get killed trying to get back."

Delvar voiced, "What about dragons?"

Captain Jacobs strode back and forth in front of us. "Yes, we get dragons occasionally—not so much here but at Midreach. I cannot impress upon you the IMPORTANCE of having a permit to cross the Dragonwall. Otherwise, crossing the wall is a one-way trip."

Obi knew what Captain Jacobs had meant, with all his talk of fool-hearty adventurers getting killed crossing the wall. He meant them. He would kill our party if we were caught crossing the wall.

Tug snickered behind Obi. "You got in trouble."

Obi ignored Tug's banter. Obi was concerned that the short trip across the wall to get Majora's box was becoming more difficult than anyone had suspected.

The captain mounted his horse. "You can take this as friendly advice, use it, and we won't have a problem."

Delvar gave a friendly smile. "Thank you, Captain. We will be moving off to Midreach in the morning."

Captain Jacobs reined his horse and went to the north portion of the wall, looking over. He pointed down and, in a gravelly voice, said, "Lieutenant, make a report of a growing limb here! We will need to return and cut it off."

Obi and Tug peeked over the wall to see the limb the captain was talking about. About twenty feet down the north face of the wall, a thin tree grew out, cracking some of the mortar and displacing the bricks around it. Obi felt sick to his stomach. He didn't want to hear any more about crossing the wall. It was becoming increasingly dangerous just to be near the Dragonwall.

Eight

Tomorrow, everything will change.

Raising his hand above his head, Captain Jacobs called out, "Let's move." The militiamen, alert to his commands, began moving down the wall. Seven more horses passed and ten men in leather. Their weapons were at the ready, their eyes fixed forward. Obi wondered if the men in leather might be light infantry in training.

The militia had moved off, slowing plodding along down the wall, well out of hearing range.

Delvar turned to the rest of the party. "Can you believe that we need a permit to cross the wall?"

Vestos sat on his pack. "A permit will take four days there and four days back, to make a one-day journey across the wall to get a box—that is, if they let us keep it. You heard Captain Jacobs. Anything suspected of being dragon magic will be destroyed."

Tug let out a huff. "That sounds all official, but I get the sense they will go through whatever treasure we find and take the best, leaving us with scraps. As for the magic, I doubt if they will destroy any of it—just keep it for themselves."

Obi could hear the truth in Tug's words. Tug had been right about Captain Jacobs at a glance and was probably right about the guards taking Majora's box.

Tark agreed. "There is another way. We stick with the original plan. We just don't get caught."

Tannon threw up his hands. "Whoa! That is your plan? Don't get caught? You heard the captain. If he catches us coming across the wall, he will shoot us. Four days to Midreach and another four back is a small price to pay to not get killed."

Tug scoffed, "We won't get killed crossing the wall, but they will take our treasure that we bring back. I guarantee that."

Obi wished he had been paying more attention to the original conversation. "What else did the captain say? You know, about what's on the other side of the Dragonwall?"

Tug growled out, "Weren't you listening? He said a lot of things besides dragons. He confirmed what Majora had said about the undead, and sometimes you can see them at night."

Obi didn't like the idea of the undead creeping around at night. He asked, "From on top of the wall, how would Captain Jacobs know if they were undead? They could just be people, trying to gather food."

Tug pointed across the wall. "Yeah, that's right. Remember the deer grazing? They didn't look skittish at all. I said it once, and I will say it again. These people are starting to believe their own stories. Nothing more than an old wives' tale."

Picking up his pack, Tark said, "The undead don't scare me, but losing a week traveling to a distant town, just to take a stroll over a wall, really pisses me off."

Vestos smiled broadly and pointed to the coils of rope, lying at the south wall where Tark had laid them. "I know why Captain Jacobs didn't believe you. He could see our wall-scaling equipment. He knew we were going over the wall."

Tark threw up his hands. "Crap! No wonder he didn't believe us. He knew we were lying!"

The party laughed at themselves. Vestos made his loud belly laugh and wiped away a tear from his eye. "I imagine we will see Captain Jacobs again."

They picked up their gear and headed down the gradual ramp. On the left-hand side stood a large fire ring with solitary logs here and there around it and a pile of wood against the Dragonwall. They moved around the ring and dropped their packs. Vestos was already unpacking his bedroll. Obi went straight to gathering kindling to build a campfire.

Delvar sat down on a piece of firewood. "Tark, I believe the Captain was telling the truth about the undead, and, if we are caught across the wall, they will use all of their means to stop us from crossing back."

Tark paced back and forth, considering his options. A serious looked etched his brow. "I too believe the captain would shoot us. That warning was clear. He seemed to get real sensitive about anything associated with dragon magic."

Tug unrolled his bedroll and grumbled, "Bah! Did you see their shinny armor? It's all flash for parading around. Who said Captain Ass was trouble? Me, that's who!"

Annoyed and frustrated, Tark said, "Yes, Tug, you did. It would be a waste of time to travel a week and a day to get the permit, just for them to take away our treasures."

Vestos sat on his bedroll and took off his boots. "Eight days to get a permit isn't good for anyone and will most certainly upset Majora."

Tark stopped pacing and said, "Okay, show of hands. Who is for getting a permit and crossing the wall?"

Tannon and Obi raised their hands.

Tark continued, "Who is for crossing the wall early morning and making it back before nightfall?"

Delvar, Tug, Layna, and Vestos raised their hands, along with Tark.

"Good. Five to two, it is settled. We go over the wall in the morning," Tark said.

Tannon shook his head. "Captain Jacobs knew we had every intention to cross the wall. I expect that he will come back tonight to chop down that limb."

Tug smirked. "It will take time for the guards to come back. They will have to wait till daybreak to find the limb. We will have lots of time to make it to the church and back before they get here."

Tannon stood with his arms crossed. "I will not go with you over the wall, not without a permit. If something goes wrong, we could get stuck over there for a very long time. We are taking a really big chance, not to mention facing the undead."

Tug teased, "Did the captain get under your skin?"

"Yes, he did. The captain and his men will kill us, if they catch us coming back over the wall," Tannon snapped.

His face turned red. Tug raised his voice. "IF! If they catch us coming back across the Dragonwall, but we will be hidden by darkness. We just need to go at dawn and come back at dusk."

Tannon waved his hands at Tug, his tone more defiant. "No! My father had a saying—don't push a bad spot. Guess what? Crossing the Dragonwall is a bad spot. There are too many unknowns, too many things that can go wrong. We will get caught or, worse, killed."

Tark seemed to sense Tannon's resolve. "How about you, Obi? Will you come with us without a permit?"

Obi felt a tinge of guilt trying to decide. He didn't want to hurt Tannon's feelings but had made a promise. "I have an obligation to Majora, to my Sovereign, and to this party. I think it wise to get a permit before crossing the wall. With or without a permit, however, I will go with the party."

Tark thought for a moment before he spoke. "Tannon, you don't have to go across the wall. You can stay here. Once we are gone, you can pull up the rope and wait for us to return."

Tannon shook his head. "No, it isn't right."

Tug gave a grin and raised an eyebrow. "I got it. We could send Tannon to get a permit. He could walk four days to Midreach, obtain a permit, and return. By that time we will have the box and be back on Majora's Island. And the best part, we split the treasure with one less!" He barked out a laugh.

Tark shot him a look for him to keep quiet. Tug's smile broadened.

Tannon's frown deepened. "No, you don't understand. I want to keep my sister safe."

A gentle hand patted Tannon on the shoulder. Layna moved closer to him, as if shielding him from the others. "It's all right, brother. I don't need you to help me go to the church. You can stay behind."

Tannon stared, trying to read her eyes.

She winked at Delvar, before feigning a somber expression to Tannon. "I will be fine. If not, you can explain to our father that you had to get a permit and could not worry about keeping me safe."

Tannon's ears turned red with frustration. He threw up his hands. "Fine! We will go in the morning. Damn it! Why are you being so foolish?"

She wrinkled her nose at him and kissed him on his cheek. "I knew I could count on you."

Tannon rolled his eyes and gave Tug a steely glare. "This is what we get hanging out with humans—rash decisions."

Tark slapped him across the shoulders. "Good. It is all settled. We leave at first light."

Tannon nodded sourly. "Tonight we can be comfortable and rested for whatever foolishness comes tomorrow."

The thought of crossing the wall tomorrow made Obi anxious. He had to do something to keep his mind busy. Obi unrolled his bedroll and pulled out the leather-bound book. He sketched a few drawings of the Dragonwall, filling in the detail he had seen as they had approached. He drew Captain Jacobs yelling at the party and a crude sketch of the valley.

Vestos was busy making meal preparations, checking herbs. "I will see if I can do Majora's herbs justice."

Layna, with Swiftwing poised on her hand, headed toward the swamp. "I am certain you will do well, Vestos. We will see if Swiftwing can get something good for dinner."

Obi hoped it would be a rabbit.

Tark and Tug began clearing the campsite of the larger rocks and wood chips. Tark announced, "Can't sleep with these boulders under my bedroll."

Although the thought of clearing the area of rocks and bark to make sleeping more comfortable was a nice gesture, Obi didn't really care. He doubted if he would sleep much tonight.

Tug joked, "Here is a fine boulder and tree limb." He tossed the rock and branch aside.

Delvar rummaged in his packs to find something for the group to eat. "Well, gentlemen, it is getting to be slim pickings. We have a biscuit, cheese, and dried fruit."

"We should finish this bacon tonight. Soon it won't be fit to eat." He tapped a biscuit on a nearby rock. "As for the biscuit, bacon grease will soften it."

Tannon returned with a large armload of firewood; he dropped it beside the fire ring. "I don't think any amount of Majora's herbs will help the biscuit."

Delvar murmured, "No, I suppose not. Perhaps Layna and Vestos will work some culinary magic."

Tannon looked confused. "What sort of magic is *culinary?*"

Obi, Vestos, and Delvar looked at each other and laughed.

Tannon barked out, "Fine! Have your laugh. I will see if my sister is better company." He turned and stomped off.

It felt good to laugh but not at the expense of a friend. Obi called, "Wait, Tannon! We meant no harm."

Tannon waved him off and continued walking away.

"Let him go, Obi," Vestos said. "Young trees are easily damaged, but they heal just as quick. He will be okay come morning. Come. Let's get this fire going. A meal will make everyone feel better."

Obi figured Vestos was right about Tannon and began sorting the firewood and restacking the piles. Vestos gathered the food items Delvar had selected for the evening meal, while Obi tended the fire.

Once assured the fire would not go out, Obi decided to go look over the wall. He climbed the gradual ramp, crossed the wall, and gazed at the valley. It was a nice-looking place, not at all scary. The wall here, as in most of the places he had looked, sloped out slightly, and should be easy to climb with a rope. At the base of the wall, the sloped pile of broken rocks—ranging from small boulders to small stones—followed the wall, like it was a part of the construction. After the rock was a gentle grassy slope with scattered trees that separated the wall from the broad river a half mile away. As far as Obi could tell, the river followed the wall. To the east and downstream was a sharp bend in the river, like a notch, and a tall outcropping of granite slate forced the river to curve toward the wall. Majora had said that, about five miles due north of the granite rock formation, was the village.

Tug had voiced how the locals believed their own stories, but Obi was not so sure. He could not believe that anyone would go to the enormous effort it took to build this wall just for a story. "No, things are not what they seem here. Majora had said it, and I had best never forget it." Obi turned away from the view of the valley and looked to the south. Layna and Tannon emerged from a small grove of trees some distance away. He hoped Layna had put Tannon in a better mood. She seemed to have that effect on her brother, cheering him up when he needed it.

Rather than stare at them as they made their way to the camp, Obi turned back to the valley. He tried to memorize landmarks, hoping this would help guide their way, once the group managed to get over the wall. Down along the face of the Dragonwall, Obi could see the tree limb that Tug wanted to use for an anchor. The limb was fairly large, about twenty feet below Obi. It looked as if it had been cut away before and the limb had regrown.

Something had changed since they had left Majora's Island. Obi could feel a growing tension in the party. They had had disagreements in the past, but this new feeling seemed more serious. A strange mix of fear and excitement washed over him. Before they stayed at Majora's Island, they were just traveling from one place to another. Camped next to the Dragonwall, the unknown adventure started right here and now. Tomorrow he would be places unknown, sights unseen, and he might even see a dragon!

After seeing one, then what? Would he leave his friends? Would they come back to Delvingdeep with him? It was a waste of energy. He would worry about such things after he had seen a dragon.

"Obi!" Tark yelled from below. "If you are going to eat, you had better come now!"

Dinner turned out to be hardtack biscuits—with a generous helping of bacon grease to soften them—and dried apple slices. Much to everyone's disappointment, Layna's owl Swiftwing had not found any rabbits. Obi looked at his biscuit doubtfully. He decided to eat it quickly to get through it, washing away the greasy taste with many pulls from his water skin. Obi lingered over the apple slices. He thought of the monastery's garden and wondered how long it would be before he would break bread with the Sovereign.

Tark finished washing down dinner with half of his water skin. "So, how do we get over the wall?"

"Just jump. Something is bound to catch you. If nothing else, there are soft rocks at the base," Tug said, grinning. "Actually Tannon had a good plan."

Tannon started slowly, prefacing any scaling with the notion of the rope being concealed from the guards. Obi listened and took note of how well everyone responded to Tannon's idea. He had incorporated Tug's idea about using the limb as a base and also concealing a rope from any guard who might be watching from the wall.

Tug raised an eyebrow. "So let me get this straight. We leave the rope behind, attached to the limb off the side of the Dragonwall? What happens if a guard comes along and chops it off?"

"If they chop off the limb, there is a chance the rope will be discovered. I will try to get the rope as close to the base of the tree and wall that they won't see it."

Tug added, "A rag soaked in mud could be wrapped around the rope. From a distance the dried mud would look like mortar and could be easily overlooked."

Tark clapped his hands together. "So it is settled. Tannon, make your preparations. I suggest we all get a good night's sleep. Tomorrow is going to be exhausting. We find the church. We get the box, and we come back. Easy!"

Delvar piped up, "Don't forget we search for treasure!"

Tug agreed. "Who really cares about Majora's box? I am looking for gold!"

Everyone seemed satisfied with Tannon's plan to maneuver the Dragonwall. Any normal banter was strangely quiet. Everyone must have realized that they were really going over the Dragonwall. The adventure would start at daybreak.

Obi lay on his bedroll. Staring up at the stars, he thought about Tannon's plan. A nervous knot formed in his stomach. Tomorrow he might see a dragon, and everything will change.

Nine

Who will go first over the Dragonwall?

Obi awoke, yawned, and stretched. He had slept well. For a brief moment, he had forgotten where he was. The feelings for the coming day flooded him with a nervous excitement. Today was going to be his first real dragon adventure. Excited to start, he got out of his bedroll and wrapped it up and secured it to his pack. He checked the journal, his crossbow, and counted his bolts.

Vestos was up. He had a crackling fire going and was heating water for the morning tea. "Good morning, Obi! Did you sleep well?"

Obi moved to warm his hands by the fire. "I did. How about you?"

"I slept well, when I slept. I was restless, so I have been up for a while," Vestos said.

Obi let out a deep sigh. "I take it you and I are not eager to dangle from a rope?"

"I actually am more worried about getting back up. Down should be easy, as long as the trip is not too fast." Vestos raised a finger. "We have a good plan. Besides Tannon will not risk his sister. He'll make sure it is safe."

Obi agreed. "Why are you worried about getting back up the wall?"

He poured Obi a cup of tea. "I have never climbed a rope so high. I am not sure if I can do it, but I guess I will have too."

Obi was thinking so much about getting down that he had not thought much about getting back. This new thought did not give him any comfort. He wished Vestos hadn't mentioned it.

Vestos patted Obi's shoulder. "Try not to worry. How hard can it be? It will certainly be easier with a full stomach."

Obi could tell Vestos was uneasy too, by the way he doted over the oats. "I am nervous about going over the wall. We are taking a lot of chances just to save a few days."

Vestos nodded in agreement. "It will be fine. I think you're just nervous and need something to do. I will get breakfast going. You go chop wood."

Vestos was right; Obi was nervous and excited. He went to the woodpile, where cords of wood had been stacked against the Dragonwall, and several split cords. He picked the splitting maul and pulled out a large round. He swung it over his head, in a large arc. The maul sank into the wood with a loud thump. He worked the maul out and swung it again. He turned the larger piece and swung, splitting off a second wedge. After the third round, he had worked up a sweat. He was glad to have work and to keep his mind occupied. He realized what Vestos had intended. By the time he had finished the eighth round, the nervousness had lessen. Obi headed back to camp.

Vestos had made breakfast and tea. The others had awakened, while Obi helped himself to a plate of food. The gruel was hot and sweet, with the subtle earthy tones of Majora's herbs.

Tannon wolfed down his breakfast. "When do we start over the wall?"

Tug finished his breakfast and smirked. "Tannon, for someone who doesn't want to break the law, you sure are in a hurry."

Tannon corrected, "I don't mind breaking the law. I just don't want to get caught. The earlier we start, the more time we have there. Did you forget Majora's warnings?"

"Oh, the one that says, we shouldn't be there at night? Yeah, I heard it." Tug waved him off.

Delvar laughed. "It seems our cautious young half-elf is wiser than you gave him credit for."

Tark clapped his hands together. "All right, enough of this banter. Let's get going!"

They followed Tannon up the ramp until they reached the top of the Dragonwall. Tannon stopped above the branch. "Delvar, head out about fifty paces. Set up watch."

Tark stopped. "Tannon, have you checked the limb, to make sure it can hold us?"

Tannon tied off the rope and tossed the rest down the side of the wall. "Yes, last night. Who's first?"

Tug reached for the rope. "Me. I will go first."

Tannon explained, "Good. After you get down, I will lower the packs. That will make it easier for the rest of us to climb down."

Tug climbed to the top of the wall with the rope in hand and, pushing out, he started his descent. He took careful strides backward, till he reached the branch, and then began moving faster. In a short time, he stood at the base.

Tannon sent down the packs, one after the other, till they all lay at the base of the hill.

Vestos nudged Obi. "The packs are down. Are you okay, Obi?"

Nerves and anxiety had a firm hold on Obi, making his hands shake. Obi could tell Vestos could see it too. Obi lied, "I am all right. Just excited to get going."

Vestos gave him a knowing nod. "I swear the wall is growing taller, and Tug is getting smaller and smaller every time I look over the wall."

Obi looked down; the wall was a two-hundred-foot drop. "I know. If you're trying to cheer me up, it isn't working."

Tark called out, "Vestos! You're up."

The thought of stepping over the wall made Obi's hands sweat. Out of the party members, Vestos was the heaviest and not eager to trust his weight to the rope. Obi tried to think of something to reassure his friend. All he could think of was, Don't fall. Instead he said, "The rope will hold."

Vestos paused, giving Obi a nod, before moving down the rope. Once he was below the limb, Vestos seem to walk down the wall in a nervous cadence. He was much slower than Tug had been. Vestos made a gradual and deliberate walk down the wall, until he made it to the bottom. Obi let out a sigh of relief.

Layna pouted. "Finally! It took him long enough."

Tannon took her by the arm. "Layna! Don't get into a rush."

She made a defiant face at him, sticking out her tongue. She took the rope and went over the side of the Dragonwall. She took long strides down, her face making it look as if she had practiced this many times.

Tannon, staring at his sister, said, "She is showing off on purpose, just because I told her to go slow."

Tark turned to Obi. "You're up."

Obi felt his heartbeat quicken. He wiped his sweaty palms on his robes.

Tannon gave Obi a loop of rope. "Are you nervous? You have climbed a rope before, right?"

His mouth was dry, but Obi stammered out, "A little bit nervous and, yes, I have."

"Good, off you go," Tannon said.

Obi could see that Tark was worried about him. Obi was determined that he would just show his friend that he wasn't afraid. He gripped the rope tightly. It was fuzzy and thick, making for a good handhold. Obi took a deep breath, summoning his courage, and rolled over the edge of the wall. He moved quickly down the rope, until he could see the limb clearly. The limb wasn't a limb at all, but a moderate-size tree, about the size of his thigh.

He glanced down. The wall was a sheer drop, and the party members down below looked like ants. He immediately regretted looking. The shock made him jump; his feet slid off the wall. His shoulder banged against the wall, threatening to break his hold. He clenched the rope as tightly as he could. He scrambled to get his feet under him but kept slipping off the wall. He froze and gripped the rope as hard as he could to avoid falling.

Tark yelled, "Stop messing around. Get down the wall!"

The only thing Obi could hear over his racing heart was Tark's irritation. Obi tried to move, but fear would not let him.

Tark grumbled out, "Tannon, see what you can do."

Several minutes later, someone tapped him on the shoulder. Obi forced his eyes open and looked up.

Tannon hung on a second rope with one hand. "We are a long ways up. Don't worry about falling. Focus on the rope. And get your feet under you, just like you're going to walk up the wall. Vestos said you would be able to do this with no problem."

With Tannon's assurance, Obi brought up his knees against the wall.

"That's great, Obi. Now stand up, and you can start going down."

Obi tried to fight back the fear; his hands began to tremble. "I am going to fall, Tannon."

Tannon gripped him by this robes. "Don't be silly. I have seen you climb a rope before."

Obi had climbed a rope—but never so high. He knew better than to let fear paralyze him. He forced his limbs to move.

"Get your feet under you," Tannon instructed.

Obi's hands were tired from gripping the rope. He worried that his hands were too fatigued to hold himself. He took a deep breath and brought his feet against the wall and stood up.

Tannon patted him on the shoulder. "Good. You will be down in no time."

Obi started downward, shuffling his feet, while slowly lowering himself. He stopped and wanted to look down, but, if he were still a long ways up, he might freeze again. Obi decided to focus on the rope, making sure he had a firm grip before he let the other hand go. His hands ached, turning stiff from chopping wood and holding tightly to the rope. It seemed like he would never get down, then his foot hit something. He was thankful it was the rocky base of the wall.

The immediate area was scattered with small flat cacti and fallen trees, and was steeper than he realized from above. Vestos nudged him. "That was a long ways down, wasn't it!"

Obi was relieved to be off the wall. "I thought I was going to die. Tannon really saved me."

Tark and Delvar descended without incident, making the trip look normal. As planned, Tannon was the last down. He pulled the rope from the wall taking the end and tying it to the base of the tree branch and pressed the rope against its base. He descended the wall as easily as Layna, making it look effortless.

Vestos, with a look of deep concern, said, "Uh, say, since you tied off the rope to the branch, how are we going to get back up from the branch to the top of the wall?"

There was a moment of stunned silence in the group. Tannon was coiling the rope he had dropped and seemed not the least concerned. "I have a grapple hook in my pack. I was wondering when you would see the small flaw in our plan. Shall we go?"

Delvar snorted. "Very funny."

The walk down to the river's edge was easy. The river was wide and slow-moving. Obi noticed it was cooler here than it had been on top of the wall. Morning had come, burning off a pale mist.

Tug stopped short of the river. "How are we going to cross it?"

Everyone paused a moment. Even though they had all seen the river, no one had thought of crossing it. Annoyed, Tark asked, "Show of hands, who can swim?"

Obi and Layna raised their hands.

Layna said, "There are many fallen trees. We take some rope and tie it to a log or two. It will give us something to hold on to, and we can put our packs on it. Then we just kick our feet, and away we go."

Obi recalled at Majora's moat how Vestos had said he wasn't good at swimming. "We could make a dugout canoe."

Tug scoffed, "We could, if we have a day or two to burn it out. Nothing like telling the guards we are here with a signal fire."

Tark raised a hand. "Tannon, Obi, head off down the river. Tug, Delvar, go upriver. See if we can find an easier way to cross."

The river current was slow, and Obi could see a long way down the river without a bridge in sight. There were many fallen trees, looking like a mud slide had knocked them down ages ago. Downriver a hundred yards on the far bank, Obi spotted the rock outcropping, the one Majora had given as a reference point. Tannon and he walked until they were certain there was no other easy way across and returned to the party.

Clapping his hands together, Tark announced, "Okay, looks like we need a tree or two large enough that we can put our packs on."

Delvar pointed. "That one is large enough for us."

Layna was quick to latch a rope along the log's length. "Together, we can drag it to the riverbank."

Obi was at the small end. The others scattered around the log and Tug pushed them from shore. The river was colder than Obi had thought possible, a sharp contrast to the cool waters of the swamp. The cold river current made his legs stiff and hard to move; his hands were turning a pale purple, and his fingernails were blue. He wished he had a pair of gloves.

Tug chatted, "Damn, this is cold water. My legs don't want to move."

Many others agreed; only Tannon and Layna didn't complain. The cold water sapped Obi's strength, but he kept kicking.

The bank crept closer, till Obi could put his feet on the riverbed. Shivering and weak, the group dragged themselves up on the north shore on the long granite boulders and stones. They pulled the log onto the bank and rested on the warm rocks.

Ten

That is not a stone.

The granite outcropping of stones was hard and warm, offering little comfort. Obi lay with the others, on his back against a large bolder, and was relieved to be off the wall and across the river safely. His hands ached from gripping the rope on the wall's descent. He flexed his fingers back and forth, until they felt better. He was surprised how the cold water had sapped his strength. He checked that his writing book was securely wrapped and dry.

Delvar was the next to stir. "As comfortable as these rocks are, I must remind everyone of Majora's warning of the nighttime danger. We really don't know how far away the town is. Perhaps we should warm ourselves on the march."

Tark raised his head. "Can't you just say, let's go?"

Delvar's grin broadened. "Words are fine things, and I like to share."

Tark shook his head and sat up. "Words are fine things, but I hate to hear you squander your riches."

Delvar jumped up and swished the cloak over his shoulder, saying, in a deep voice, "Let's go! Adventure awaits, and I am impatient to greet her!"

Waving a hand, Tark said, "Fine, you can lead the way."

"What? Really? Uh, right then. This way. Come on." Delvar climbed down the rocks and began marching north.

Everyone stiffly followed. The rocky ground slowly gained height and turned into gently rolling hills covered in waist-high field grass. Small trees stood scattered through the valley and denser in the low spots were outcrops of bushes. Birds called from the trees and chased insects through the grass.

They crossed several small game trails. In many places along the slope, colorful wildflowers grew in large patches. Behind them, the river stretched out far to the east and west, revealing a lush landscape. Beyond the river, the Dragonwall etched the horizon, rising up from the valley.

Vestos let out a whistle. "This place is beautiful!"

Layna agreed. "This land hardly seems to deserve the reputation that it has been given."

Vestos exclaimed, "You're right. This area would make great farmland or pastureland for cattle. Why are people afraid to settle here?"

Layna pondered, "This whole valley can be seen from the Dragonwall. They must know how perfect it is. How could they not explore and settle here?"

"It's possible that they have explored and found reasons to stay south of the wall," Tark interrupted. "Whatever the cause, everyone said not to be on this side of the wall at night. I don't want to be here to find out."

Layna plucked a yellow flower. "It's so beautiful. We should stop and have a picnic."

Tark shot her a look, which she ignored. "No time for picnics. Let's keep moving. The sooner we find this 'lost' village, the longer we have to look for Majora's box and any other treasure."

Delvar swished his cloak and marched off, taking the lead and setting a good pace. The sun rose in the sky, and the day grew hot. The hills became taller and steeper. Obi was getting tired. He had stopped admiring the fields and trees, and, to keep from stumbling, he focused on looking where he was walking.

Delvar took advantage of the terrain by following game trails to avoid the brush. The trail made for easier walking, making switchbacks up the steeper portions of hills. Obi noticed the occasional white stones that stood out from the other rocks and dirt. At first he thought nothing of it. To pass the time, Obi would kick a white stone down the trail making it into a game. Occasionally Layna would join in to kick the white stone too. After a small break, he picked up a round stone and examined it more closely. It was lighter than he thought it would be and varied from stark white to a brownish yellow. They came in all shapes but rarely larger than a walnut. "Vestos, have you ever seen stone like this?"

Vestos rubbed the stone with his thumb. "Where did you get it?"

"They are all over," Obi said.

Vestos dug at it with his nail. "It looks like bone to me, Obi. Maybe an old deer bone?"

"I suppose, but there are so many of them. Besides I would expect that I would see bigger bones. You know, something more complete."

"Well, if they are very old, maybe time has worn them down." Vestos shrugged and turned away to continue walking.

Obi put the stone in his pocket and followed behind the rest of them, puzzling over the bone. To pass the time, he began looking for the white stones. Shortly he found larger and larger fragments. Finally he found one large enough and complete enough to show it wasn't a stone after all. He called to Vestos.

Vestos gave him a smile. "I'll be damned! It is a bone."

Obi kicked over a white bone down the trail. "Why do you suppose there are so many bones here?"

Vestos wiped his sweaty brow. "Oh, who knows? Perhaps it is always like this. You just now noticed."

Obi considered what Vestos had said; perhaps he did just notice it. Another mystery to add to a long list of curiosities.

Tark stopped at the top of a hill and sat down under a shade tree. "Water break."

Tug flopped down next to him. "No argument from me. It's getting damn hot."

The rest of the group gathered around the hilltop, taking advantage of the view and the shade. Obi shared his discovery of the bone and the many fragments he had seen.

"I've noticed those." Layna took the bone, examining it. "But I didn't think anything of it. This looks like a leg bone, but, from what, I do not know."

Grabbing it from Layna, Tannon rubbed his finger on the bone. "It seems to be very old."

Her red-rimmed eyes searched the area. Layna's curiosity was taking hold, her look of annoyance to her brother giving way to a more focused look. "Are there more bones?"

Obi pointed down the hill. "Everywhere."

Layna let out an excited giggle. "Let's go see if we can find out what they are!"

Tannon shook his head. "Layna, really? They are just bones. What does it matter what they were?"

"Brother, you are so dull. You are never curious about anything!" Layna turned away in a huff. "Come, Obi. We will solve this mystery."

Obi was glad that someone else was interested in the bones. He hated not knowing the reason for things. He joined Layna, as she trooped down the hill, searching for larger fragments. She picked up one, then another. They found several small ones, like the ones Obi had been kicking on the trail. These small bones seemed to hide under clumps of brush. Obi could see Layna was becoming impatient and frustrated. He began to think that perhaps it would have been better to not mention the puzzle at all.

Out of frustration, Layna kicked a moss-covered stone. The rock, nearly round, came up out of the ground and rolled a short distance. Obi saw a flash of white and Layna's look of surprise. She hurried over to the stone. "Look at this, Obi. It is a big one!"

"That is the largest so far! Good job, Layna."

Layna easily picked up the large stone and scraped off the moss covering.

Obi caught his breath. The stone was not a stone at all but an ancient skull; it was yellowed and cracked, the dark eye sockets filled with dirt.

"That's amazing!" Layna brushed more dirt and moss from the skull. Obi quietly reached into the hole in the dirt and pulled out the mandible, handing it to her.

Layna, quietly examining the bone, brushed off more dirt and slid the lower jawbone back and forth, till it lined up. "This was no ordinary skull."

The skull had a heavy ridge that ran from the eyes, over the top of the skull, along the back to its spine. It resembled a man's skull, but the teeth were large and pointed with wicked long fangs. Once together, the upper and lower jaw looked like it had too many teeth in its mouth. Obi asked, "What kind of creature is it?"

Layna shook the skull, cleaning off more dirt and ancient grime. "I don't know."

Obi examined the surrounding area. He could make out several of the odd moss-covered stones. On impulse he nudged one, and it rolled, revealing teeth, a jawbone, and a bit of leather.

He pushed over a few more. On the forth mound a smaller skull emerged, more human-looking. Obi soon realized that there were mounds all around him, hundreds perhaps thousands nearby. He called, "Vestos, Tark, we found something!"

Layna pushed over a few more of the moss-covered stones. Tark and Vestos came down the hill, the others following behind.

"What have you found, Layna?" Tannon asked in a bored tone.

She held up the fanged skull and stuck her tongue out at her brother. She mocked, "Oh, nothing important."

Tannon gave her a disgusted look. "Whoa, what is that? A mask?"

Annoyed, Layna made a face. "It's not a mask. It's a skull. They are all round."

The men stared around them, beginning to see the odd shapes at the foot of the hill for what they were. Soon everyone was poking and turning over rocks and sticks and logs. More bones were found and rusted ancient swords, axes, piles of what may have been spears or daggers, bits of armor.

"You have found a battlefield!" Vestos exclaimed.

Tug dropped the rusted ax head. "It does not bode well to disturb the dead."

Layna ignored him. "Yes, that must be it! The number of bones, the weapons—this proves there was a dragon war!"

Tannon doubted it. "Hold on, sister. Your imagination is getting ahead of you. Some bones in a field do not mean the Dragon War happened."

Layna thrust a skull at him. "Do all of your neighbors have teeth like this? How silly of me! Of course we bury our dead in shallow graves of random hills."

Tannon threw up his hands. "That's not what I meant. A battlefield, yes, but we can't say that this is proof of the Dragon War!"

"It really doesn't matter," Tark interrupted. "We didn't come here to find a battlefield. We need to get moving and find the village."

"Fine!" Layna tossed the skull to her brother and stomped off.

Vestos gave a pinched look. "She has quite the temper."

Tannon shook his head. "You have no idea."

Obi carefully placed the skull he was holding back where he found it. He saw Tug do the same with the skull that Layna had thrown at Tannon. Obi raised an eyebrow toward Tug.

Tug growled back, "What! Show a little respect for the dead!" Tug didn't wait for Obi to speak but promptly trotted to catch up with the others.

Eleven

What made those claw marks?

Delvar's pace had remained steady. They traveled over hills, through small patches of trees and scrub brush, and followed game trails where convenient. By the time the sun was nearly to its zenith, they stopped in the shade of a larger crop of trees atop a hill.

Although tired of walking, Obi was excited. He had faced the first hurdle, by descending the Dragonwall, and the second, by crossing the river. He wondered what else he would find on this adventure. Obi smiled to himself in anticipation, as he sat on his pack with his back against a tree.

Everyone dropped their packs in a circle and sat down. Not wanting to get caught off guard, Layna went to scout out the patch of trees. Tug wiped the sweat off his brow. "Obi, why are you smiling?"

Obi didn't realize he was still smiling. He wanted to say something profound, something to get the attention off him. "How far do you think we have come?"

Tug shook his head. "Too damn far. We need to find this village soon. I am getting tired of walking."

Running through the forest, Layna exclaimed, "I think we found it! I see a building on the next hill over. Come on, come on!"

Tannon dashed after her. "Layna, wait! Wait for us!"

The rest of the party forgot their fatigue for a moment, scrambling to grab their packs, and chased after the siblings. They found Layna and Tannon on the far side of the hill in the edge of the tree line, waiting for everyone to catch up.

A large rodent den sat just outside of town, about four feet round with torn-up vegetation. Layna moved their party around the den for a better look. There, about a quarter mile away, across a low gully, sat scattered stone foundations and a single stone building.

Tark clapped his hands. "Finally we have found the church! Come on. We can rest when we get there."

The first two recognizable foundations were little more than stone pads with rubbled walls and collapsed roofs, long ago abandoned. They passed four larger stone pads overgrown with tall grass, reminding Obi of the marsh grasses near Majora's Island.

The game trails made weaving patterns in the grass, streaking from the town to the forest, and, in many areas, the grass had been torn up in large circles. Off to the right of the church sat a second burrow, four feet wide with larger tracks around it and torn patches of grass. Dark succulent vines with white trumpet flowers competed with the rodent population to claim everything civilized.

Tark pointed to Delvar and Layna to take point and head for the church. Delvar nodded back and moved ahead. He cleared his throat before announcing in a loud voice, "This was a thriving city, and now all that is left is that church and our goal."

Vestos agreed. "If it were not for the lurking undead and dragons that inhabit this area."

Tug ridiculed, "Stories! Just rat nests and badger holes. I have not seen any undead or dragons. Perhaps they have moved off or turned to dust like most of this town?"

Clearly impatient, Tark spoke, "Majora has made it quite clear that we should not be here in the dark. I know we are tired. Stay focused. Let's get to that church, get the box, and get out."

Majora didn't make the comment lightly. Her tone was not of caution but an urgent warning with an unmistakable ring of truth. Obi knew Tark was right and could see the others knew it too; their expressions took on a serious tone.

The church stood apart from the rubble. It looked as old as the rest of the buildings but with no sign that time had claimed it. The front doors stood tall with high arched peaks and stone columns. The stained-glass windows were boarded up.

Obi wanted to point out that the boarded-up windows looked like they were trying to keep something or someone out. A look from Tark made him keep quiet.

Tug pointed to the top of the large peaked door. "I think that is a claw mark. It has five deep gouges through the wood and stone along the top portion of doorway."

Tark yelled out, "Bloody hell! What made those marks?"

Tug raised his hand, trying to reach the marks. "Am I close?"

"No, you still have a spear length to reach them." Tark clapped his hands again. "Focus. Let's not wait around and find out what made them."

Tannon grabbed the front door, tried to open it. It held. He pulled out a pick and a flat-ended piece of wire, and plugged both into the keyhole. He wiggled them, then turned them around, till a small click sounded. He pulled open the door. "There might be traps."

Tark discounted the warning and walked into the church. Seeing it was safe, the rest followed. It took a moment for their eyes to adjust from the bright sunlight to the dark building.

Slivers of light beams shone through the spaces between the boards covering the windows. A tall ceiling with wooden rafters lined the upper portion, obscuring anything lurking in the attic. A thin layer of dust covered the dark wood floor. Matching long benches lay scattered around the room, obviously scavenged to place over the stained-glass windows, turning the church into a battlement. At the far end of the room stood a raised wooden area where a stone pedestal sat.

Tark waved the rest over. "Just as Majora had said, a stone altar on a raised platform."

Delvar and Tug quickly dragged the pedestal off the wooden stage, exposing a slate gray stone slab.

Tannon pulled out a piece of white cotton cloth and brushed the dust off the outline of a hidden compartment. He opened it. A small coffer lay inside the marble box.

The chest, made of bone and silver, had ornate carvings and runes etched along its sides and placed squarely on top were carved skulls and symbols that made Obi cringe. Tug ran his fingers around the box, looking to pry it open, when Tannon spoke up. "It looks booby-trapped. I would be careful."

Tug jerked his hands back. "No one said anything about traps."

Tannon gave no hint of a smile, just winked at Layna, who smiled back at him.

Looking slightly embarrassed, Tug cleared his throat, as a warning to Tannon and to the rest of the party. "Do I need to remind you that we need to be out of here by nightfall or bad things are supposed to happen? Besides I do not want to cross that cold-ass river at night."

Obi didn't need to be reminded; he was very aware that the sun had already peaked and was heading down. Time was running out, and Majora's warning was ringing in his ears. "Is there anything I can do to help?"

Tannon took off his glove, and ran a finger gently along the rim and lightly along the edge of the box, then along the lip. He pointed his finger, tracing along the edge. "Do you see it?"

Obi didn't see anything, but, at Tannon's assurance, Obi looked again. A small plate held against each side of the box. He wondered how Tannon had seen it just at a glance. Obi wanted to ask more questions but didn't want to distract Tannon.

Tannon studied the raised platform before moving to the box, then carefully looked at the stone pedestal. Afterward he retraced the coffer's lines, gently running his fingers along its edge.

Obi tried to see what Tannon was looking for but saw nothing out of the ordinary.

He pointed for Obi to look closer at the chest's base. "See these here? There are four plates, one on each side of the coffer."

The plates were remarkably thin and blended into the box's ornate carvings. Obi watched Tannon tease them away from the coffer, immediately returning to the coffer's side. Obi said, "I have a couple crossbow bolts, and we can use them to wedge in there. Well, that is if you think it will work."

Tannon looked concerned. "Those plates will move back and forth. When the box is moved, they will come together and set off the trap. Your bolt idea might work, but that isn't what worries me."

The idea of a box valuable enough to need a trap was exciting. Not knowing what would happen if it went off was worrisome. Obi realized he was holding his breath. "What worries you?"

Sitting back on his heels, Tannon cocked his head, examining the hole. "This is what I am seeing. One plate would set off the trap. Two is overtrapping, but four plates are excessive. I think the plates are a distraction, and the real pressure plate is underneath the coffer."

Obi could see Tannon's point. "Oh, that is tricky—a pressure plate underneath the chest. So, if we move the box, it will set off the trap. What are we going to do now?"

Vestos leaned over and closed his eyes, seemingly releasing some unseen magical energy. "I can feel the magic this box contains. It is quite strong."

Obi was going to look away, but Vestos was so intent. This was the first time he had seen someone perform magic. Obi could almost sense the magic Vestos was wielding, but it could be mistaken for meditating. It didn't look like magic at all, from what Obi thought magic was supposed to look like.

In a sudden start, Vestos's eyes popped open wide. "Necromancy! The box contains strong necromancy magic, the magic of the dead."

Obi didn't like the sound of *necromancy*. It sounded dangerous. He took a step back. "The coffer contains dead magic?"

Vestos smiled. "Ah, my young friend, the magic I mean is necromancy. It is a type of magic. But you are quite right, it draws energy from the negative plane. The same magic that makes the undead come alive or vampires crave blood. They crave what they lack, a life force."

Tug rolled his eyes. "Life force? That don't mean squat, if we can't get this coffer out of here."

Obi ran his fingers through his hair. "In some of the books I have read at the monastery, they tell of a device called a trap pin."

Tannon raised an eyebrow to Obi. Tannon looked as if he was going to say something but stopped himself.

Vestos made a small frown. "What is a trap pin exactly?"

Obi thought for a moment before speaking. "I think it is a block of wood or metal key that is placed in a secret spot. So the person who returns to get the box, he can set the trap pin and get the treasure without setting off the trap."

Tannon gave him a surprised look. "That is a trade secret, but you're right. Look around for a keyhole or loose stone. Many times they are hidden in plain sight or hidden away from the trap. It might take us all day to find the trap pin. It is all depending on how clever the trap-maker is."

Tark leaned over, looking at the coffer. "You two keep thinking about how to get that chest out. The rest of us will look for the trap pin."

Tug smirked. "What the hell does a trap pin look like? I wouldn't know one if it fell on me."

Vestos raised a knowing finger. "A loose stone or keyhole that can easily be overlooked. The more elaborate the trap, the better hidden the trap pin."

Tug gave a half smile to Vestos. "You don't know either, do you?"

"Nope."

Tug cleared his throat. "Why can't we just smash it or deliberately set it off? It isn't like we are sneaking in here. Everyone here is long dead."

Tark perked up. "That is a valid point, Tug. Why are we worried about a trap that sets off an alarm? For that matter, no one has been here for a hundred years. Nothing alive, that is."

Everyone looked at Tug, considering his question, and then looked to Tannon for the answer.

Tannon shook his head. "I will give you a good answer. These pressure plates that are over a hundred years old still move smoothly. If these all move like they are new, there is a good notion that the rest of the trap works well too."

Tug snickered. "To set off an alarm? Who is going to hear it?"

Vestos raised a finger. "There is magic at work here. This building should be rubble, like the others, but it isn't. This box contains strong magic, strong enough to keep this place looking new for the last hundred or more years. I am hoping it is just a mechanical trap and not one of magic."

Everyone fell silent. Finally Tark gave a nervous chuckle. "Good answer."

Obi didn't like the idea of a trap, especially a magical trap. He didn't want to be in the church anymore; he wished they were already heading back across the wall.

Tannon rubbed his hands together. "Okay, I've got a plan. Delvar and Tug will hold back the plates with their fingers. Vestos will snatch out the box, and Obi will stuff in the bolts to hold the plates."

Tark nodded in agreement. "I like this plan. Delvar, Tug, get into position. We will go as soon as Obi has his bolts ready."

Obi took a small string, lashing his bolts together, making sure they were just the right length as the box. He double-checked it again. "Okay, I am ready."

Vestos pushed up his sleeves, giving his hands less hindrance, and rubbed his hands quickly together. "I am ready too. Here we go."

Tug piped up, "Do you want me to count?"
Vestos nodded.
Tug began, "Three, two, one. GO!"

Vestos pulled out the box, smashing Delvar's fingers. He yanked back, shaking his hands. "Ouch, son of a bitch!"

The plates quickly moving to fill the void, Obi stuffed the sticks into the hole, pushing the plates back into position.

Everyone froze, looking at the hole, and shocked the plan had worked. Tannon let his plates go. "Good save, Obi. You got those in the nick of time. Any closer and the trap would have gone off."

Tark patted Obi on the back. "Quick hands!"

Obi felt a little embarrassed by the attention given to him and could feel his ears turning red. He cleared his throat. "Just doing my part."

Vestos set down the box. "Who wants to carry this box?"

With his pack open, Tannon blurted out, "I have lots of room in mine."

Vestos took a towel from his pack and wrapped it tightly around the box. Then he tied it up with a piece of leather cord before placing it in Tannon's pack. "The box might be a little awkward in your pack."

Tannon adjusted the straps and shook his pack back and forth. "It will do."

Once he was certain the box was safe, Vestos turned his attention to the stone pedestal. He ran his hand along its edges and felt the base. "That is a fine piece of stone craftsmanship. If we had more time, I would gladly take that back with us."

Obi looked surprised at even considering moving the stone pedestal across the room, let alone across the river and up the Dragonwall.

Tark clapped his hands. "We have a small window of time to get back to the rope before nightfall. If you want to look around, make it quick."

Vestos and Delvar took to knocking on walls, the floor, and ceiling, listening for hollow spots.

Tug and Tannon took the other side of the room, examining the pews placed along the walls, looking for hidden compartments, something left behind. Obi was happy to watch the raised pedestal and wondered what exactly the trap would have done if it had gone off. He examined the inside, where the box had been resting for several hundred years. He couldn't help but wonder how Majora had known it was here all this time.

Layna shrugged. "All of this searching around has made Swiftwing hungry! I'm going outside to catch rabbits."

Swiftwing looked content sitting in the rafters, watching what was going on. Obi suspected Layna was getting bored with the mundane searching.

Tannon, grabbing the front door, said, "Here, sister, I will go with you."

Tannon opened the door. A small click sounded. Time slowed to a crawl. A small golden flash of light lit up the doorway, moving across the entire room like a wave of liquid sloshing in a bucket too small to contain it. The liquid light rushed through the air, changing shape from one wall to the next. Charged with a magical energy, the evolving light washed over the party members, enveloping them in a golden luster. The liquid emulsion rolled through the air from one person to the next, bathed them in golden magic, so fast that no one could even move. Each person was caught midheartbeat; Layna was frozen in a silent scream. The illuminating wave sloshed against Obi; he could feel the cold magic etched of death.

Vestos was right; it was a magical trap, and the magic felt like death's touch washing across him. It felt so cold, as cold as the grave. Time had no meaning. It was impossible to determine if time were moving forward or standing still. The magic was old, powerful, and scary. Obi wished he were anywhere but where he stood.

As quickly as the liquid light came into being, it winked out, leaving the church dark and deathly quiet. Layna fell to the ground. Tannon fell beside her. Tark, Vestos, and Delvar took a stumbling step before crumpling to the ground.

Obi felt his knees give out; the gritty floor slammed against his face. Majora's warning rang loudly. *Be across the wall by nightfall.* He tried to keep his eyes open, but the magic was putting him to sleep. He tried to think of how he might be able to close the door, but he couldn't move. His eyes closed, sleep quickly approaching. A dwindling thought came. *The door is open. It will be night soon, and the undead will find us.*

Twelve

Two weeks since crossing the Dragonwall.

It had been two weeks since Obi had returned from across the Dragonwall. Impressed with Obi and his friends, the Sovereign was throwing a special celebration in their honor.

A multitude of colorful banners lined the inner courtyard; a special meal was being prepared, and even the elder brothers personally congratulated Obi on his accomplishment.

He quietly made his way up the stairway to his quarters. He lit a lantern and sank down on his mat. The three bells chimed, which signaled the end of afternoon Mass, and he had an hour before the celebration dinner would start. To busy himself, he gathered three books that needed repair and headed to the library.

Obi walked down the long hallway, past the inner courtyard, to the main library entrance. He was surprised that the library curator was not at his station and that the door sat ajar. Obi pushed open the door.

A feeling of profound dread gripped him, making it difficult to breathe. The horrific sight made his knees weak. This was not the library's normal condition of pristine order but utter chaos. Books lay tossed into careless piles. Some lay open, cracking their spines. Large bookshelves lay on their sides, broken into small shards barely recognizable as shelves. Large piles of torn-out pages scattered every hallway. Huge mounds of books lay open with other books stacked on them. Large shelves that held the grand tomes were barren. All the work he had done to keep the library books in good repair had been undone. Everywhere he turned, more books were torn up, pages ripped out, some burned. Large tears rolled down his cheeks. Obi cried out, "Oh, no! Who could have done such a horrible thing?"

"Excuse me, Initiate Oberon. May I have a word with you?"

Obi recognized the voice immediately; it was the Sovereign, and it felt as if Obi had not seen his Sovereign in many days. Wiping the tears from his eyes, Obi gave a slight bow. "Yes Sovereign, I really don't know who would mishandle these books. It is so disrespectful. Let me put these away, and I will be right with you."

The Sovereign looked tired, with dark circles under his eyes that gave him a haunted appearance. He nodded ever-so-slightly. "Oberon, this can't wait."

Obi pulled a few books out of the stack and quickly put them in numerical order. "I don't know who made such a mess. Give me a little time, and I will have the library back in order."

The Sovereign's voice cracked; he cleared his throat. Obi knew the Sovereign was becoming impatient. Obi set down the stack of books and turned his full attention to the Sovereign. He gave him a deep bow. "Yes, Sovereign."

The Sovereign's gray robes made him look more like an initiate than the Sovereign of the monastery. He sat on a small bench, wiping off a red wine stain on the front of his robes, but more disturbing was his intense expression. His voice careful and deliberate, he said, "Do you enjoy living here at the monastery?"

Obi had not seen the Sovereign look so sorrowful than he did right now. Obi nodded. "Yes, sir. I really enjoy it. I have friends here. I enjoy taking care of the books."

The Sovereign dabbed a rag and wiped the stain. "That is good. Did you enjoy your trip across the Dragonwall?"

Obi looked a bit puzzled. "It was very exciting and a little spooky at times. But I always tried to conduct myself with courage and understanding, like you have taught me."

The Sovereign sneezed, wiping his nose with the rag. "Obi, you are in danger."

Obi looked at him blankly. "Sir?"

The Sovereign's expression deepened from a concern to worry, and his face turned a ghostly pale with dark circles under his eyes. He looked bad, worse than Obi thought possible. His Sovereign's face became more and more pale.

Obi could see the Sovereign was not feeling well at all and needed to rest. Obi stammered out, "Sir, I don't understand. What danger am I in?"

His voice cracked. "You're in a perilous land, far away from the monastery."

The red wine spill on the Sovereign had enlarged, covering the front of his robe and his lap. Obi didn't see any danger, just a library of books that needed to be organized and put away. "Sir?"

The library doors blew open; a hot wind tore through the library with the stench of rotting meat.

The Sovereign's face drained of color, and dark blood oozed from his eyes and nose. A hot wind blew sand into Obi's face, stinging his eyes. He squeezed his eyelids tightly together, trying to keep out the sand.

The Sovereign held a frightful and haunted expression. His voice echoed, as if he were on the other side of a great canyon. "Obi, you're still in the church."

Obi didn't understand; the only church he could recall was from a few weeks ago, picking up the box for Majora. A lingering finger of death crept along his back, making him shiver. He recalled that feeling; it was the same feeling of the shiny golden light that had went off at the doorway. "I am in the church? I'm in the church."

The Sovereign's face turned ghastly pale, blood dripping off fleshy bits across his robes. The wine stain was not wine at all, but he was bleeding through his robes. Blood smeared across his face and chest. Blood trickled from his eyes. "Wake up, Obi! You're still in the church. The door is open!"

Obi tried shielding his eyes from the harsh wind and stinging sand. The smell of hot putrid meat permeated the entire area with the stench of death. He had to cover his nose. The bright colors of the books faded into a gray stone prison cell. Obi glanced up, trying to discover what was making the stench. He realized the foul smell was coming from the Sovereign. He was rotting from the inside out.

The Sovereign's eyes blackened and shriveled, the left eye gone, replaced with a mass of writhing maggots. His dark gray robes rotted with holes and dried blood. The Sovereign made a loud belly laugh.

Fear gripped Obi like a vise. Feelings of dread, death, and misery washed over him. His Sovereign was changing into something undead right before Obi's eyes. He tried not to look, but the gruesome image held him. Obi forced his legs to move away.

The undead Sovereign lunged forward, trying to grab Obi. He scrambled away, falling over a pile of books. The zombie lunged again.

Obi tried to spring away, but his foot slipped on blood. He fell to the ground and began scrambling; the Sovereign landed on Obi. Hand over hand the Sovereign climbed up, till he covered Obi, pinning him to the ground. Obi struggled, getting his hand across the undead Sovereign's face.

The putrid flesh fell off the Sovereign's face, leaving a stark-white skull. Obi tried to fight him off, but he was too heavy, too strong. His rotting teeth bit into Obi's chest, tearing out large chucks of muscle and bone.

Obi tried to fight but found his arms
paralyzed. Blood ran from his neck, draining away his
life's essence. Obi knew he could not come out of
this alive. A feeling of profound calm came over him.
He began to float upward. Soon he was looking down
over his body; he found it difficult to keep his eyes
open, and his own mortality was coming to an end.
His blood drained in large pools. The monastery floor
melted away to be replaced with a brown wooden
floor covered in gritty dust.

Obi awoke from his nightmare, the images of
the undead Sovereign still playing out in his mind's
eye. The nightmarish feeling of death clung to him
like honey trying to force him back to sleep. Obi
pushed himself up into a sitting position. The
gossamer ropes that held him slowly fell away, until
he was fully awake. Obi didn't recognize where he
was. Dark brown floors with high ceilings and rafters.
Long benches scattered about the room and boarded-
up stained-glass windows. He was still in the church.
He was still behind the Dragonwall and still in
dangerous lands. He was where he had fallen when
the golden light had washed over him. The church
door stood wide open, letting in the warm air.

Delvar, Tark, Tannon, Vestos, and Layna lay
sprawled out on dark church floor, as if they were
dead. Recalling the Sovereign's warning, Obi
mumbled, "We are in danger. We are still in the
church."

Tark yawned, stretched, and rubbed his neck. "Damn, I am sore. That is what I get for sleeping in my armor. I really don't know how you do it, Delvar."

Vestos jumped to his feet. "We are still in the church!"

A mass of panic swept through the party. Tark rolled to his feet and drew his sword. Delvar, Tug, and Tannon did the same.

Tark stood tall, brandishing his sword high above his head. "What the hell was that light? How long were we out? A few minutes?"

Vestos dusted off his robes. "I believe so. Did you feel the touch of death?"

Tug sheathed his short sword. "The feeling of death clings to me like a cold blanket. It felt like it wanted to keep me asleep, with so many nightmares."

Vestos continued, "That light was necromancy magic woven into the trap."

Tark shook his head in disbelief, trying to rid himself of that feeling. "It was the same feeling I got when my brother had died so many years ago. The same feeling when the plague swept through the City of Kings. Thousands of people were dying in the streets, in gutters. The whole city stunk of death."

Layna shrieked out, "Swiftwing! Where is Swiftwing?"

Tark held up his hand. "Calm down. We will find her."

She put two fingers in her mouth, making a loud whistle.

Obi tried to shake the feeling of the magical trap. The nightmare it had sparked in him left him feeling a bit shaken and disoriented. "How long have we been out? Is it the same day?"

Tark commented, "A few minutes, I think."

Layna picked up something on the ground, the unmistaken form of a rabbit carcass. She plucked it up and examined it. "See these marks? Swiftwing caught this rabbit. We have been out for more than a minute or two, more like an hour or more."

Tark refused to believe it. "What! No, it can't be!"

Shaking the rabbit at Tark's face, Layna yelled back, "No, much longer! Swiftwing had time to go to the field, catch a rabbit, and bring it back. Even on a good day, it takes an hour."

Tark nodded absently and muttered a curse under his breath.

Delvar thumped on the wall. "I am going to check out the inside wall. I want the treasure."

Tug called out, "We might as well stay the night here and use the church as a barricade against the undead, and then head back at first light. Besides, it will allow us to search the entire area for gold."

Obi did not like the idea of staying the night on this side of the Dragonwall. This side was dangerous, and Majora had warned them. She had said, if they had to stay the night, to hide until sunrise. Obi didn't like disobeying the party, but he found himself determined. He would not stay the night here, even if it meant leaving the party and coming back for them in the morning.

Vestos eyed Obi. "If we do stay, we run the risk of getting caught or, worse, stranded here."

Tannon glanced at his sister. "All of this arguing is burning the precious time. I am with Vestos. We make it back. If anyone has forgotten, we do not have a permit, so we risk getting killed coming over the wall."

Still shaken from the nightmare, Obi said, "Tark, I don't want to stay here."

Tark clapped his hands together. "It is settled then. We should go back to the wall tonight."

Obi vigorously nodded his approval. "We should go now."

Delvar threw up his hands. "Whoa! Hold on there. We are here now. We should search this place first. We have an opportunity staring us in the face. This church is a safe place behind the wall. This place had one secret spot. Perhaps there are more hidden areas filled with treasure."

Tug agreed. "Tark, we have come this far. We should get what we can."

Tark took a deep breath, considering Tug's concern, before answering, "That was my intent too, to search this place for an hour before heading back, but that trap put us an hour behind. Majora knew about the box, and she says there is undead here."

Tug scoffed, "Since we have been here, we haven't seen any undead. The night doesn't scare me. Why should it scare you?"

Tark made a fist. "Hell, that trap was over a hundred years old, and it went off. I believe Majora. She knew where the box was, and she gave us a warning not to be caught across the wall at night. You and Delvar can stay over here, if you want. The rest of us are heading back."

Tug's face flushed with anger. "At least give me some time to search."

Tark huffed out, "Search now. Tear this place apart, and be quick about it. As soon as Layna finds Swiftwing, we are going."

Wasting no more time chatting, Tug tossed the pews about, checking the walls, slamming a large fist against them. He moved quickly, thumping and rapping on anything that might conceal a prize. Obi felt certain that, if given more time, Tug and Delvar would tear down the church looking for treasure.

Layna walked to the door and gave another low whistle, calling for Swiftwing. "If I were to hide something of value, I would simply put it in the rafters. Perhaps up at the peak, hard to reach, and easily spotted, if you know where to look."

Tannon gave her a wide smile. "See? My sister is very crafty."

Vestos rubbed a finger along his temple and said, "Not much light up there. You will have to be as graceful as a cat to make that climb."

Tannon grabbed a large bench, still intact. "Obi, give me a hand to prop it up."

Obi didn't want to stay the night in the church and worried about making it back alone; he silently cursed himself for being rash. He helped Tannon to prop the bench against the wall. Obi held it. Tannon, using it like a ladder, walked straight to the rafters.

Obi tried to peer into the darkness without success. "A lantern would be helpful."

Tannon carefully stepped from one rafter to the next, plodding along. "It's too dark up here. I can't see a damn thing."

"A lantern, you say?" Delvar stopped thumping and tossed his pack to Vestos.

Vestos retrieved a medium-size lantern from Delvar's pack. "Perhaps I can shed some light up there."

Obi recognized the lantern; it was the same lantern that Majora had put in the barn. Vestos soon had the lantern shining brightly and held it out, splaying its light into the rafters.

Tannon called out, "I think I see something."

Tannon moved gracefully along the rafters to the far wall, retrieving a small leather bag. He placed it in his mouth and dropped down to the floor. "Here you go."

Delvar tipped his head to Tannon. "You can move quite fast when properly motivated."

Tannon shrugged. "Just want to make it back before nightfall."

Clapping his hands, Tark spoke. "Let's get moving. We will have to move faster than before to make it out before nightfall."

Delvar made a sweeping gesture with this cloak. "I will make sure we set a good pace to make it back in time."

Layna made a low whistle, as she looked at the skyline. Like a shadow rising into the sky, Swiftwing came from the fields, making a wide circle, coming to rest on Layna's outstretched arm. "Now we can go."

Tark checked his sword. "Delvar take point. Let's move."

Tug rolled his eyes. "Between Delvar with his cloak and that owl, I don't know who makes the bigger performance."

The sun hung low in the sky as the party left the old village and made for the hill where they had first seen the church. With each step Obi felt better leaving that retched place and hoped he would never see it again. At the base of a hill, Obi looked back and cringed. The church, with its high arched peaks and stone columns, glowed red, as if painted in fresh blood.

Thirteen

What are those things?

At the top of the next hill, the group caught up with Delvar, who had gotten ahead of everyone. They found him with his shoulders slumped, and his cockiness gone. The party gathered around him.

"Delvar, what is the matter? Why are you stopping?" Layna asked.

"We can't make it," he said quietly.

Layna urged, "Sure we can. We just have to walk faster."

"No, Layna, that's not it. We have company. I think they are the undead." Delvar pointed down the hill along the tree line. There, moving swiftly in the underbrush, were several pale manlike creatures. They darted from tree to tree, pausing only to peer out at the party.

"Oh, shit," Tug muttered.

Delvar continued, "They are blocking the way to the Dragonwall. In the trees, they can come at us from all directions. They will surround and swarm us ..."

"Shit, shit, shit," Tug repeated.

Obi stared down at the tree line for a moment. He tried to get a sense of what they were. They were shorter than the swamp people and moved quite fast, making a shrieking wail when they stopped.

Tark voiced, "Delvar's right. We can't go down there. We have to go back. The church is the most defensible place we know. We will take our chances there and make it back tomorrow morning."

Obi couldn't believe what he was hearing. It made him sick to his stomach to think of spending the night in that old church. *It will be dark soon*, Obi thought. He might be able to break into a run and try to make it back over the Dragonwall before it got dark. Even if he did make it to the Dragonwall, he doubted if the rest of the party would be able to keep up, especially those in armor. He looked around, searching for something at the top of this lonely hill that would make this nightmare go away.

"Obi, OBI!" Tark shook him. "We can't stay here, and we dare not risk the woods at night. We have to go back."

Obi's mind raced; he could make it to the Dragonwall. He could run past the undead creatures, cross the river, and climb the rope. He bit his lip, considering his option.

Tark stood face-to-face with Obi, a look of anger in his eyes. "Obi, move your ass!"

Obi had made a promise to Tark not to compromise the party or put them in danger. Obi didn't like this choice one bit, but the decision was made. He didn't like it, but he would keep his word. Obi scanned the area before pulling out his weapon. He cranked as fast as he could on his crossbow, but he still took long enough for Tug to comment, "Have you considered something quicker, like drowning your opponent?"

The fighters drew their respective weapons, while Tannon drew his short sword, and Layna readied her sling. Vestos pulled open the decorated sheath, revealing a bright sliver spear tip.

Obi loaded his crossbow with a thick quarrel, raised it to his shoulder. "It may be slow, but it's got reach."

Tug raised a doubtful eyebrow. "If you hit your target."

Obi shrugged. The crossbow was what he had; besides, he would much rather fight at a distance than up close. He wasn't armored like the fighters, Tug, Delvar, and Tark.

Tark called out, "Stick together, so we can cover each other's backs."

The group ran down the hill, back toward the church. It seemed to Obi that the sun was setting ever faster now. As they reached the bottom of the hill, it was getting difficult to see very far into the tree line. Feelings of panic began to well inside him. They scrambled up the next hill. Obi thought he saw something moving in the brush. "I think those things are following us."

Layna paused to glance back.

Tark gave Layna a firm push. "Keep moving!"

Tug growled. "I don't like this. We are being herded. I know it!"

Tark spurred them onward, till they reached the edge of the village clearing. The church's bloody-red hue faded, leaving it gray and dark, with the front door already ajar. "I know. So we better get to the church before those things do!"

Obi could see the door was not shut, but something else was wrong. He thought he had seen something move from one of the windows. He wanted to stop running to get a better look but didn't want to be caught by those things behind him. Then from a second window he was certain he had seen a pale figure look out and darted back in. Something was inside the church, and Tug was almost there. Obi shouted, "Tug, no!"

Tug ran to the door. "Come on. We need to barricade—"

The doors kicked open. The first creature jumped high, locking its hands around Tug's throat and putting its feet in his midsection. Tug went down, the monster standing on his chest. Tall, thin pale men charged out of the church toward the party.

Delvar jumped back, crying out in alarm. Two more creatures, same as the first, charged Delvar and Tark.

Fear made Obi freeze. He tried to look away, to move, but all he could do was stare. The creatures were like men but hideous and twisted. Their thin, naked bodies were pale blue and gray; their features, sharp and angular. Their chins and ears were long and pointed, but their noses were nothing but gaping holes above a black mouth filled with sharp triangular teeth. They did not speak but shrieked and hissed as they charged forward. Their clawed hands and feet tore great clumps of moss from the ground.

Tark dodged the creature that charged him, while he slashed at it, tearing across its chest. Delvar went down under his monster's attack. He rolled backward, over his shoulders. He kicked out with both feet, catching the monster square in the chest. Tossing it high into the air, the shrieking creature landed heavily at Obi's feet.

Frightened, Obi fired his crossbow. The bolt hit the monster right at the base of its throat. To his horror it only seemed to drive the thing into a wild frenzy. Pinned to the ground with Obi's arrow through the back of its neck, it tore at its own throat. Its legs flailed, as it beat clawed feet into the moss, crying a high-pitched scream.

Obi would have continued to stare, but Vestos shoved him around. Looking up and turning, he saw more of the creatures coming. A mass of thin, pale monsters ran into the village clearing from the brush.

"Get to the church!" Vestos yelled.

Obi ran passed the thrashing monster, as it tore itself loose from the ground.

Yelling a guttural battle cry, Delvar swung a terrific overhand blow and hit the monster right on top of the head, splitting it to Obi's bolt. Obi ran to where Tug struggled with the monster on his chest. Tug held the creature's jaws at bay with a firm one-handed grip on its throat and slammed his blade into the beast's side. The monster was not deterred by the great slashes Tug's sword opened in its side; its grip on Tug's throat did not weaken. Without thinking, Obi swung his crossbow as hard as he could. The iron stirrup on the end of the crossbow caught the monster right on the side of the head, crushing it like an eggshell. Black blood sprayed across Tug's chest and face. Tug kicked the flaying body away from him.

Obi yanked Tug to his feet and jerked him toward the church door.

Tug snarled at him, "Clear the church."

Layna ran past Obi, headed for the church doors. Layna screamed, "Delvar, Tark, get to the church!"

Tannon took off after her. "Layna, wait!"

Obi looked first at the church and then at Tark, Delvar, and Vestos. The three were backing up toward the church, facing the creatures tearing across the courtyard with more emerging from the burrow. Tark had killed the third monster that Obi had seen him dodge, his blade dripping with the creature's blood. Tug, on the other hand, charged to meet the monsters. Obi thought Tug must be enraged by the pain of his wounds, or perhaps he was just crazy.

Tark yelled, "Tug, stay back, damn it!"

Delvar stopped his retreat, advancing on the next monster leaping at him. "Tark, help him!"

Tark screamed obscenities and stepped up to the monster in front of him.

"Obi, shoot the damn thing!" Tannon yelled.

Obi stared at the crossbow in his hands and quickly began to crank the string back. He tried to ignore the rushing monsters advancing on the church. He slipped the bolt in place and raised the bow to his shoulder.

Vestos made a gesture with his hands, and, with his right, he pointed at a monster trying to flank Tark. A brilliant beam enveloped his hand and shot out, hitting the monster in the face. The creature's head shattered, just like the one that Obi had hit with the bow.

Obi cursed under his breath. He didn't know Vestos could do that.

The effect on the monsters was encouraging as well. They appeared startled and confused.

Obi took advantage of the creature's hesitation and aimed at one of the two monsters facing Tug. Obi fired and saw the bolt hit the creature squarely in the chest. It was knocked back a pace; the bolt tore a hole through its chest, but it did not fall. Obi hurried to reload even as he tried to comprehend what he had just seen. It wasn't possible; the bolt went straight through the monster's thin frame. Was the crossbow useless against them? But what else could he do? He had little choice but to try again. Obi sighted down his bow. A moment later he saw Tug decapitate the unwounded monster he faced. The thing's headless body took a few steps, stumbling into the fiend that Obi had shot.

Tark's terrific slash severed a clawed hand from another beast, spraying dark blood as it spun away. Delvar too was successful in running his opponent through the throat.

To Obi's dismay, neither of these wounds seemed to slow the monsters any more than his bolt had.

There were seven monsters, one each battling the warriors, and four more creeping up, looking for an opening. Obi had an inspiration. He fired his next bolt at the head of one of the distant monsters. He missed and in a moment of regret realized that the four were now turning their attention to him. Struggling to reload, Obi yelled, "The head! Hit them in the head!"

Vestos, armed with a spear, charged to help Tark. The creature that Delvar had stabbed just ignored the sword and had grabbed Delvar's forearm with both claws. With a yell Delvar pulled the creature toward him and simultaneously gave a powerful kick to its chest. The thin beast flew backward, completely off Delvar's sword, and landed a few feet away.

Whether he heard Obi or not, Tug slashed at the second monster and hit it in the temple, shearing off the top of its head. It fell like a puppet whose strings had been cut.

Vestos stabbed the monster he and Tark battled in the face. The spear entered through its eye socket and lodged in its head. Tark turned and ran. "Vestos, run!"

Seeing an opportunity, Delvar grabbed Tug by the shoulder. "Run before they regroup. We stand at the church."

Obi thought that Tug would not run from battle. He had a snarl on his face and a wild look in his eye. Surprised, Obi saw Tug had turned with Delvar, and they ran for the door.

Obi stepped aside, letting Delvar and Tug run by. He saw Vestos was struggling with his spear. Obi picked the nearest monster and fired his crossbow. The bolt hit the monster low in the pelvis. It did not stop coming, but it slowed down. Obi screamed, "Vestos, leave it!"

Tark skidded to a halt at the door and shoved Obi through the doors. "Vestos is right behind me. Get inside and get ready to bar the doors."

Vestos had freed his spear and was running with a monster on his heels. Obi tossed his crossbow down and reached for the doors. Vestos came flying headlong through the threshold, a monster attached high on his back. Together they crashed to the floor.

Tark jumped over a tangle of broken pews toward Vestos, while yelling at Obi, "Close the doors!"

Obi slammed his shoulder into the door, and Tug did the other.

The monsters outside crashed into the stout barricade. Tug and Obi were almost knocked away, as the doors opened and slammed shut. Obi cried out, "Tannon, help!"

Tannon placed his shoulder on the gap of both doors, and they held when the monsters hit them again.

Layna wedged a solid pew against the door that Obi held. "Help Tark and Vestos."

"No, get more pews! Bar the door!" Tannon yelled.

Obi looked to see that Tark had backed the creature away from Vestos and was trying to cut it down. Vestos had not moved from where he lay.

Obi grabbed another pew and rammed it against the door Tug held. Obi yelled, "Tannon, we have this. Guard the windows!"

Tannon ran for the most open of the windows.

The monsters outside hit the doors again, but with the pews and Tug and Obi holding them, the doors didn't budge. Obi chanced a look over his shoulder to see where the other monster was and what was happening.

He saw Layna throw a board at the creature's head; it missed. That was all the distraction that Tark needed; he slashed the creature across the back of the knee, causing it to stumble and fall. Tark's powerful backswing hit the monster in the face, nearly cutting its head in half. It slumped over backward and lay still.

Fourteen

Everyone is yelling.

Outside, penetrating shrieks and moaning signaled that the ghouls had the party trapped. Through the tangle of broken pews nailed to the shattered stained-glass windows, gray claws reached into the church windows, trying to catch anyone close enough to pull them through.

Tug yelled to watch the windows, even as gray claws scratched and clawed at the barricades trying to get in. Delvar, heaving more pews up against windows, ranted in a constant string of swear words. With everyone at yelling at once, Obi couldn't make out what anyone was saying. All of the shouts and screams turned into a loud roar of words.

Out of the shrill cries and yelling, Tark shouted louder than the rest. "Shut up! Shut up!"

The shrieking from outside chilled Obi to the bone. He didn't say anything but scrambled over to Vestos. Blood covered the floor where Vestos's head lay, and Obi could see bloody rips on the back of his friend's robe. Vestos moaned. Relieved, Obi gently helped him into a sitting position. "I am glad you're alive!"

Vestos grimaced in pain. "I almost made it."

Vestos's wounds needed tending, but the clawed monsters were still trying to enter the church. Obi gave him a pat and stood up. "I have to help the others."

Vestos's head wobbled and looked frailer with each passing moment. "Go. Go. I'm fine."

Obi looked for a window to help barricade.

From behind him, Tug said, "Hey, Vestos. You look like shit."

Vestos waved a feeble hand gesture. "Still better-looking than you."

Obi turned on Tug, ready with angry words for someone who would make fun of a wounded man. His anger died out when he saw the state Tug was in. He stood hunched over, covered in his own blood, plus the nasty black blood of the creatures. He had cuts along his neck where the creature had grabbed him, and there were rends in the chest and midsection of his armor.

Not knowing what to say, Obi turned away and grabbed a pew, dragging it over to one of the windows. He and Layna wedged it against the closed shutters.

Everything got quiet inside the church; only the sound of heavy breathing broke the silence. It was very different outside; the creatures shrieked and wailed, making shrill calls and moans. It seemed to Obi as if they were calling to their kindred.

Tannon grabbed a broken pew, pulling it over to another stained-glass window. "What are those things?"

Delvar answered, "I think they were ghouls. I heard a tale back in Delvingdeep of undead scavengers. They feed on anything, but it is the grave-robbing meals that turn them vile."

Obi recalled reading about ghouls back in the great library. When he had read about them, he had thought they were a myth but recalled that they might be afraid of fire.

Outside, the shrieking grew louder, as more ghouls surrounded the church.

Obi would tell the others about his fire idea once the fighting calmed down.

Loud thumps and scrapes sounded against the double doors and windows. The doors held, but Obi could see that the windows would not. There were far too many windows and far too many ghouls. A gray claw thrust though an opening, tearing away a section of the barricade.

Layna cried out, "They are going to get in!"

Tark hacked at a clawed hand, loping off several fingers. "I see that."

Across the room, Tug called out, "The roof! We can defend the roof!"

Obi ran to the leaning pew that Tannon had used to get into the rafters. He scrambled up the makeshift ladder. It was darker now than it had been earlier. It took a moment for his eyes to adjust, but he didn't have time to wait. He hammered his fist against the roof; it didn't give. The church was well constructed, and then he began to think they were truly trapped.

He could hear the fighting and cursing of his friends below. Scrambling along the rafters, thumping against the roof looking for a weak spot, he found a loose board. He hammered on the board with all his strength. It moved, but it wasn't enough. Desperate, Obi held the rafter in his hands, flipped upside down and kicked the roof with both feet. Two boards smashed and fell out. It was not a big hole, but it would do. "Come on. We can make it to the roof from here."

The fighting was intense around the windows, but they were holding their own. Vestos and Tug were covering one window each. The others were covering at least two, each slashing and stabbing to keep the ghouls from entering.

Obi scrambled down to Vestos, realizing that he would need help to get to the roof.

Vestos put an arm over Obi's shoulders and grabbed him around the waist. Together they made it to the bench leaned against the wall. Obi said, "I will go first, then help you up."

Obi climbed up; Vestos waited a moment before making an attempt. Obi grabbed Vestos by the pack and hauled him into the rafters. He climbed out and helped Vestos on to the roof. Outside, Obi could see more creatures moving around in the shadows of the old village. If they gained the rooftop, the group was doomed. "You okay?"

Vestos gave him a wave. "I got it. Go."

Obi swung down into the church again. His eyes had adjusted to the dim light, and he could see a lull in the fighting. Layna was moving more pews and broken wood into place to reinforce the barricades on the windows, while the warriors guarded the more open spaces from attack. Obi helped Layna wedge a pew against another shuttered window. Obi called, "Tug, can you make it to the roof?"

Tug ran to the makeshift ladder. The pew wobbled and shifted under his weight. He growled out, "Of course I can."

The ghouls threw themselves at the doors and windows, using their mass of bodies to force open the barricades.

Tark and Delvar took the two remaining unblocked windows. Tannon, armed with his bow, stood in the center of the church launching arrows at the uncovered windows.

Obi picked up Vestos's fallen spear and stabbed through the gaps in a window. It bit into a ghoul; it twisted in his hands. He pulled back and thrust, again and again.

The ghouls kept coming forward, making ear-piercing shrieks and clawing their way past the barricades. Layna made her way, window to window, putting up reinforcements where she could.

Tark and Delvar swung heavy chops, cutting down the ghouls as they tried to enter the windows, severing limbs, hands, and occasionally a skull top, spewing black blood into the air.

Obi was becoming tired, and he could see Tark and Delvar were too. Their blade swings had slowed down; their chops were exceedingly heavy and slow.

As quickly as the clamor had started, most of the ghouls retreated, leaving a few fallen, plus their blood splattered across the walls and floor.

Tark roared out, "Quick, before they come back! Everyone, get to the roof."

"I'll go last." Obi amazed himself for being so brave.

Tark began to argue, but Obi cut him off. "I have Vestos's spear. I can use it to knock over the pew after I come up."

Tark nodded. "Right! That makes sense. Good plan, Obi."

Tannon followed Layna onto the roof and then the others too.

The doors boomed as the remaining ghouls hurled themselves against the barricades. Loud crunching glass and splintering wood erupted around the windows and doors. The ghouls tore through the barricaded windows, pushing their way into the church.

The shutters and pews were torn away, as the ghouls burst through a window below. Obi used the butt of the spear to push over the pew. He called out, "There are more than before."

The falling pew crashed against the floor, making a loud thump, getting the attention of one ghoul. It squatted on all fours in the center of the church and bound across the floor as more of its fellows clawed their way through other windows. Obi scrambled from the rafters through the hole and on to the roof. Tark and Tannon yanked on his robes and pack to help him up. The ghoul below was joined by others. Once they realized there was no resistance at the windows, they had rushed in.

Obi's feet slid through the hole; the ghoul leaped for him but fell short. It tried again, but the rafters were too high to reach.

Tannon let loose an arrow, striking true in the creature's face. The ghoul made a horrific shriek, mixed with anger and pain. It fell backward. The other ghouls set upon it, immediately tearing it apart.

Tannon was shocked. "Can you believe what they just did? That's crazy. They ate him."

Horrified by their cannibalistic behavior, Obi realized, if he had been slower climbing up the pew, they would have caught and eaten him.

"Hell, shoot more of them!" Tug cried. "We should kill them all. Better they eat each other than us."

Disgusting as it was, Obi completely agreed. They all did.

Tark moved up to a steep section of the roof. "I think so too, but I don't think we can. There are too many. What we need to do is survive. Tannon, shoot a couple ghouls, then get away from the hole. Maybe they will be distracted enough to leave us alone."

Tug didn't look happy about the decision but nodded his agreement.

Tannon handed a fistful of arrows to Layna, then stood over the opening, drew his bow, and fired. Quickly Layna handed him another arrow, and he fired again. After four arrows he stepped back.

A roar of tearing flesh and shrieks, punctuated with screeching and the sound of crunching bones, ensued. Obi tried not to think about what was happening below or what would happen to them if the ghouls took the roof.

Tark sat down at the edge of the roof to watch the ghouls circle. "Good job, Tannon. The rest of you spread out. Make sure we can see all sides of the church. I don't want to get ambushed, if they find another way up."

Layna sat next to the opening in the roof; at her side was Tannon. "I will cover the entry."

The others were dead tired. Tug and Vestos lay so still that Obi feared they had died, until Tug coughed. Obi lay down on the other side of the roof. He felt exhausted; his arms and legs were heavy. If the fight came now to the roof, all would be lost.

Fifteen
Sleep will be impossible.

The ghouls had surrounded the church, while others crept though its interior. The high-pitched shrieks had stopped, replaced by low moaning. The sounds were not very loud, but they were constant and carried with them the expression of a dreadful existence. Occasionally the moaning was punctuated by sudden snarling, shrieks, and wailing, before returning to the low moaning.

The fighting in the church had been terrible, but the waiting on the roof and the not knowing when the next attack would come was worse, the worst part of waiting. Obi could hear the ghouls' claws scrape the walls, as they tried to find a way to the roof. The wooden fragments and benches were knocked over, and sometimes he heard the heavy thump of a ghoul leaping for the rafters.

The lingering moaning started to wear down Obi's resolve. He slid to the edge of the roof and peeked over. The moon had come out, and Obi was able to get a better look at the savage undead. Now that the party was out of their sight, the ghouls seemed dimly aware that they had been chasing them.

After studying them, Obi realized that there were both male and female ghouls. Most had little or no hair covering their gray skin, and all were nearly naked. The articles of clothing that they did have on were nothing more than rags that hung on bony frames. He found it difficult to tell the ghouls apart, because the identifiable parts were so emaciated and shrunk to nonexistence. Their limbs were long and thin; both their hands and feet ended in thick, sharp black talons.

Occasionally one would look up in the moonlight. Obi could see the sharp triangular teeth surrounded by black lips. The worst part was their eyes—little more than round black pearls in eye sockets which gave them a hollow expression. Obi thought the ghouls might know what they once were and were aware of what they had become. The look of sorrow, misery, and despair quickly gave way to a maniacal bloodthirsty rage, when they caught sight of a living being. Obi turned away. "Tark, how do you think we can get out of this?"

Tark looked exhausted and struggled to keep a civil attitude. He gave Obi a worried look. "I don't know. If the ghouls leave in the morning, then we will just run for the wall. If not, well, that will be a different plan."

Obi hadn't considered staying until morning. He wanted to get away and make a run for the Dragonwall. "We should go now and lose the ghouls in the dark."

"Don't think we can. Vestos and Tug are wounded and will be moving slow. And we are outnumbered three to one. In the morning we will see if they move off, or, if need be, we can drive them off."

Obi didn't like the sound of driving them off. He was too tired to attempt much fighting. "I remember reading that the ghouls, the undead, are afraid of fire. Maybe we should try that."

Tark nodded. "Good to know. The fighting has stopped for now. We need to regroup. We will have two watches tonight. Tannon, Layna, and I will take the first watch. You and Delvar can take the second. Vestos and Tug are to rest tonight. Get what rest you can. Tomorrow will be a long day."

Obi nodded and slipped away from the roof's edge and went to where Delvar was cleaning his cloak. He noticed Delvar's normal flamboyance had left him, replaced with a serious expression. Obi said, "We will have two watches. You and I will take last watch."

Delvar thought for a moment and then wrapped himself up in his cloak. "Wake me when it's time."

Obi stared at Delvar, not believing that he was going to sleep. How could anyone get any rest with that constant ghoul moaning? Obi turned away and moved quietly to where Vestos lay. "How are you doing? Would you like some water?"

Vestos gave a weak smile. "I have been ill-used. At the moment, coming over the wall seems like a bad idea. No water. I just need to rest. Weaving magic takes more effort than it looks. Would you do me a service?"

Obi nodded, unsure what his friend might want. "Yes, of course, anything."

Vestos fumbled with the pockets in his robe and pulled free a folded packet. He held it out. "Put this packet in my water skin. It won't be hot, but we will have tea in the morning."

Obi was shocked. "How can you think of tea now? We are trapped on a roof surrounded by the undead."

Vestos's smile didn't fade. "Life goes on, and it will be better with something in our bellies. Get into my pack. You can soak the oats overnight for the morning gruel. Use all the honey I have left. It will taste better that way."

Obi nodded and searched Vestos's pack, pulled out the water skin, and added the tea packet. He dug around for Vestos's little cauldron and the oats he kept. Obi found the remaining honey and oats, and added both to the pot, and realized he didn't have enough water to soak them. Vestos rambled on until he had fallen asleep.

Obi didn't pay attention to what Vestos had said but did admire his attitude. Vestos was wounded and surrounded, yet he was moving forward, planning the next day like it was any other. Obi vowed to remember his friend's resolute attitude.

Obi moved away to look over the side of the church. The ghouls were quiet now, making low moans and haunting growls. He surmised that they had forgotten about the party and were wandering in large circles around the church. He climbed up a steep section and made his way across the rooftop to where Tug lay. "How are you doing?"

Tug shifted around far enough to glare at him. "Unbelievable! How do you think I am doing?"

Obi tried to mimic his rough tone. "Well, you look like shit!"

With a flash of anger Tug's eyes snapped open and then softened. "I'm sorry, Obi. I feel bad, true enough. That ghoul was damn quick. I knew better than to let him get that close."

Obi joked, "It wasn't waiting for an invitation for you to kill it."

Tug barked out a laugh. "I guess not."

Obi offered his water skin to Tug, who quickly grabbed it and growled his thanks.

Even in the dim moonlight, Obi could see Tug's wounds looked infected, with raised welts and blood smeared over his armor. "While we have a chance, we should clean up those wounds."

Tug glared at Obi over the water skin. "Yeah, I know."

Obi pulled out a clean scarf, soaked it with what remained in the water skin. "This might sting."

Tug grabbed the scarf. "You're not going to nursemaid me. I got this."

"Get some rest, if you can." Obi left him to tend his wounds and made his way to Layna and Tannon.

The siblings talked quietly in their elven language, pausing as Obi approached. Tannon's frown didn't soften, but Layna smiled at Obi.

Obi told them of Tark's plan and letting Vestos and Tug rest. Tannon's frown deepened to a fierce scowl. Layna replied, "That will be fine. I don't know if any of us will be able to rest tonight."

Obi asked, "I was wondering if you had any extra water. I gave mine to Vestos and Tug. I wanted to soak the oats for the morning gruel."

"Eating is hardly important—" Tannon began.

Layna smiled again and put her hand on Tannon's arm. "Of course, Obi. How thoughtful. I have an extra skin in my pack. I think it is full."

Obi tried to ignore Tannon's angry gaze, as he retrieved the water skin from her pack. "This will do nicely—"

Tannon cut him off. "We should focus on getting through the night!"

Obi tried to keep Vestos's idea of *life goes on.* "We will get through the night."

Tannon's expression darkened to anger, then he snapped, "What makes you so sure?"

Obi wanted to say something profound but couldn't think of anything to express Vestos's ideals.

Layna put a gentle arm on Tannon. "See, brother? Even the young races see no point in brooding on bad things."

Tannon's eyes looked angry but also frustrated. "But …"

Her soothing tone made Obi feel better. Layna continued, "But what? We will get through the night, have breakfast, and leave. Don't worry about anything else."

Obi excused himself, leaving Layna to talk to her moody brother. Obi thought it odd. Tannon was very protective of his sister; yet, in many ways, he needed her more now than she needed him.

Obi poured enough water to cover the oats and suspected their group would run out of water by tomorrow. He lay back against the roof and tried to rest. Obi realized the more quiet the party became, the louder the moaning seemed. After a short try, Obi concluded he would not be able to sleep, so he would try to meditate like he had been taught in the monastery.

The Sovereign had often pointed out that the calm mind guided the body and an agitated mind was no guide at all. Obi focused on an image of the library books on the shelves near a desk where he often worked. He slowed and controlled his breathing, trying to ignore the low moaning and shrieks from below. Darkness seemed to swallow him.

Someone touched his shoulder. Obi woke with a startle. Tannon loomed over him with a finger pressed against his lips, urging him to be quiet.

Obi rubbed his eyes; the low moaning was still present, but it was not as loud. The moon had risen high in the sky, illuminating the rooftop. "What's happening?"

"It's your watch. As long as we stay out of sight, the ghouls seem to have lost track of us being here. I will go wake Delvar."

Tannon was very light on his feet, and his footfalls were masked by his leather boots. He moved silently across the roof to Delvar. Layna lay on her back with Swiftwing perched upon her knee. The owl's head swiveled around to stare at Obi.

He cranked back the heavy string of his crossbow, making loud clicks. It had never seemed to be as noisy as it was now; Tannon's bow seemed more and more attractive. Obi shifted his position closer to the entryway.

Looking over the remains of the ruined village, he could see the ghouls lurking, avoiding the bright moonlight—a comforting thought. If the ghouls didn't like the moonlight, then surely daylight would drive them back to whatever hole they had emerged from.

Delvar, with a short bow in hand, took a position lower on the roof, giving them crossfire positions about the roof opening.

Tark shuffled along the rooftop straight to Obi. "I have a plan that might get us out of here. We'll attack the ghouls with fire. If the fire does not drive them off, I think we need to try to escape just after first light."

Obi felt a wash of relief; it was good to plan. "So, what do you want me to do?"

Tark pointed in Delvar's direction. "We have some flasks of lantern oil. Delvar has a lantern. Help him get it lit. It's the safest way to have a fire up here. Once we have that, I will get everyone up and plan our escape. It will be light then, and we will know if we have to fight our way out."

Obi had known Tark would come up with a plan; he was always able to think on his feet. Obi said, "The ghouls don't like the moonlight. I think they will leave when the sun comes up."

"Obi, I surely hope so." Tark moved away toward Tannon and Layna.

Obi made sure the lantern had oil, and struck the flint and steel, causing a bright flash. He tried it again. On the fourth attempt, a tiny hot spark ignited the wick and created a small flame.

When Tark returned, he was grinning and carrying several flasks of oil, which he set down near the roof opening. Layna, with Tannon trailing behind her, came close. She whispered, "Vestos and Tug are asleep."

Tark rubbed his hands together. "We have noticed the ghouls avoid the moonlight. I think they avoid any light. So I planned on roping a few of the church pews, pulling them up on the roof, and dropping them over the side. We will use the oil and make a large bonfire."

Layna looked puzzled. "A bonfire? Oh, I see, to act as a diversion so we can run."

Tark nodded. "That is it! A diversion so we can run for the river. If we outdistance the ghouls, we will be that much ahead of them by sunrise."

Tannon shook his head. "I don't think a little fire will drive them away. When they get excited, they charge forward. Then they are no longer by the fire."

Obi agreed. "No matter how sad and desperate the ghouls appear when calm, as soon as they have prey, they turn bloodthirsty."

Delvar looked over the edge of the church. "Why not just wait till sunrise?"

Tark cleared his throat, visibly uneasy. "We have a long distance to cover, and a few of us are wounded, and the rest of us haven't had any sleep. I am trying to give us as much time as possible to get back to the Dragonwall before sunset."

Obi understood what Tark was trying to do. No one had slept much since crossing the wall, and the coming day would be hard to keep a fast pace.

Delvar rolled a hand across his mustache. "Why can't we just stay up here for another day? We could fortify this place when the ghouls leave. That would give us more time to look for treasure."

Tark gave a pinched look. "We can't stay on this roof very long. We have little water left, and no shade from the sun. Spending the day up here would waste our strength. Our best chance is to leave now."

Layna looked eastward. "The sunrise is still a ways off. We should wait for dawn, then go."

Obi listened to them argue and was worried that the ghouls might take notice. Tark was steadfast on leaving sooner than later, and Delvar and Layna focused on waiting for sunrise. Their discussion went back and forth, their voices becoming louder and louder.

The ghouls took notice; a few shrieks sounded, echoed by others. Their moans were higher-pitched. They were circling back toward the church.

Tark thrust a finger at Delvar. "Listen, we should go. Use the distraction and make a run for the Dragonwall."

Delvar argued, "You're not listening to me! We should wait for sunrise! We have plenty of time to make it back."

Tark shouted, "The wounded, the fatigued, we are going to be slow! Not to mention the rope will be discovered sometime today."

Steadfast Delvar said, "You don't know that! We should wait for the sunrise. They can't move as fast."

Layna hissed, "Quiet down, both of you! You're going to wake the sleeping and piss off the ghouls."

The shrieks became more frequent, calling more of their kind to the church. Obi looked over the side. Out of the darkness more had arrived than he could easily count. Their moans and shrieks were louder and sounded more terrifying, more desperate to find them.

Tug rolled to his feet, making a loud thump.

Even in the darkness of the rooftop, Obi could see that Tug was out of his mind with fever. His eyes were half closed and sunken in, with dark circles etched around them; his skin was considerably paler than before.

Tug roared out, "GET OFF ME, YOU SONS-OF-BITCHES!"

"Be quiet," Tark began.

Tug let out a battle cry and charged his friends, drawing his sword as he came. "I'll cut you all down!"

Tark grabbed Tug's arms, as he crashed into the group. Obi, holding the lantern, turned away, trying to avoid the two men. They slammed into Obi, pitching him forward.

Obi sprawled out, trying to catch his balance. He hit hard and slid down the roof, knocking into Layna's feet, which kicked over the flasks. The three oil flasks quickly skittered down the roof disappearing down the hole. Layna tried to keep her footing by stutter-stepping and landed on Obi's hand. He jerked his hand back, letting go of the lantern.

The lantern skittered across the roof and down the hole. Layna fell next to Obi, and together they slid to the edge. Tannon scrambled to snag one of Layna's ankles, and Layna grabbed Obi's belt. Obi stopped short of the hole.

The flasks of oil shattered on the pew. The lantern followed suit, breaking and starting a fire, sending a blast of heat that blew through the roof's opening. Obi stared for a moment, watching the fire spread across the old dry pews, growing and spreading along the back wall. The dry benches and debris caught fire quickly. Several of the ghouls shrieked out in surprise and anger. Obi was certain things had just gotten worse.

Sixteen

Somewhere between the frying pan and the fire.

The fire spread along the pews, broken benches, window fragments, and torn-up barricades, and licked the wooden braces holding up the roof. Obi scrambled for a handhold to keep from falling into the burning heap. He was thankful for Layna's and Tannon's quick reflexes in grabbing him.

Tark and Delvar wrestled with Tug. Delvar tripped Tug, and the three of them fell hard, making the whole roof shake. Tug let out an explosive breath of air, as the wind was knocked out of him. Looking bewildered, Tug tried to catch his breath. "What are you doing?"

Delvar, still clutching his arm, said, "I would think you should tell us! Waving your sword around like that."

Tug gasped out, "I ... was ... dreaming."

"Well, you are safe with us," Tark yelled.

Vestos pointed out the smoke rising up from the hole. "You are as safe AS us. Unfortunately, by the smell of the fire, none of us are safe for very long."

Tark clenched his teeth. "Oh, what the hell? What happened?"

"When the three of you bashed into Obi, the lantern went downstairs and nearly Obi along with it," Vestos recounted.

Tark stood up. "Whether you like it or not, it is time to go."

Tannon snapped back, "Have you forgotten about the things that chased us up here?"

Tark's eyes flared. "You can become a hot meal for these monsters! I prefer to die with my sword in hand!"

Obi was glad to see Vestos was not as bad off as Obi had thought. His friend had dark circles under his eyes and looked weak but had better color in his face.

Vestos acknowledged Obi with a weak grin. "We should look for a way out of this that does not involve our early demise."

Tark looked down at the fire. "Here is the plan. We need to move now! Walk along the rafters away from the fire. The flames have driven out some of the ghouls. We can hold the church until the fire forces us out."

Tark climbed onto a rafter. One by one each party member followed him through the hole and made their way along the rafters away from the fire. Obi knew they had little choice. The fire was quickly spreading; it wouldn't be long before they would be trapped. He grabbed his gear and threw on his pack. Without thinking he grabbed the pot of oatmeal. Obi was the last to scramble onto the rafters.

The fire had spread across the pews and benches. Hot smoke was collecting along the roof. The heat made him wince and stung his eyes, making it difficult to see. He covered his mouth with his sleeve, using it to filter the smoke. Blinking hard to force back the tears, he moved as quickly as he could along the rafters to the rest of the party.

Obi could see that most of the ghouls had left the burning building, leaving a few stubborn ones lurking in the shadows. Their shrieking had changed to a hissing and moaning in frustration and surprise.

Tark called out, "Get ready!"

Get ready for what? Through the smoke and his watering eyes, Obi realized that Tug and Delvar were going to leap down from the rafters into the few remaining ghouls.

Tug jumped down with his sword raised high, bringing the blade on top of a ghoul's head, splitting it to its breastbone. Both crashed to the floor. Delvar dropped farther away and rolled up to his feet. Two ghouls lurking in the shadows made a menacing shrill and leaped at him. He hacked at the ghouls, giving Tark time to hang and drop.

Coughing and gagging, Obi lost track of the three men. Acrid smoke stung his eyes, forcing them to shut. Whether he wanted to or not, he had to get down. Squinting, he didn't see any ghouls. He slid off the rafter, using one hand to help slow his fall, and clutched the cauldron with the other. He landed; his feet slipped, and he landed on his butt. The crackling fire echoed with the clanging of metal and the shrieking ghouls, which made it difficult to hear anything.

Why the hell am I worried about the cauldron? But Obi knew why—it was Vestos's, and it was more than a pot. It was a symbol of his friend's spirit. Obi rolled to his feet.

The ghoul came around the corner; it had a black mouth full of razor-sharp teeth, and a bloodlust burned in its black-pearl eyes. It crouched to leap at him. Being this close, Obi could smell its foul breath and noticed it was missing three fingers, which oozed.

Fear made a cold sweat break out across his brow. Obi looked for a place to run. If he did run, the ghoul would climb on his back, like the one did to Vestos. No, Obi would have to stand his ground and face the beast. Obi took a step back and swung the only thing he had, the cauldron. He gripped it around the handle, poised to strike. The ghoul with black mouth and sharp teeth launched forward. Obi dodged its claws, bringing up the pot, hitting the ghoul on the side of the head with a resounding clang, knocking it off its feet. To Obi's amazement the thing leaped upright and came for him, again hissing and spitting. Obi spun in a full circle, swinging the pot low then high, bringing it up just under the chin of the drooling beast. It sprawled backward, landed hard, flailing about, trying to get to its feet.

Obi could not hear the moaning, shrieking, or even the crackling of the fire, only the sound of the blood pounding in his ears. He leaped forward, swinging the pot in a great arc over his head. He brought it down on the ghoul's skull, making a loud crack. The ghoul went limp.

The smoke-filled church made it hard to see more than a few feet. Obi turned to check for others but saw only Tug, pale and sweating. He was leaned on his sword like a cane. "Well, I see you have found something quicker than a crossbow."

Vestos, Layna, and Tannon appeared out of the smoke. Tannon coughed. "We have to get out of here! This place is coming down."

From the churches double doors, Tark called to them. "Over here."

Delvar and Tark had killed the remaining ghouls, but Tark had paid for it with a nasty cut above his right eye. A thick line of blood ran down the side of his face. Tark grabbed the door handle. "All right, we are going to open these doors and fight our way out of here. We make for that hill where we turned around last night. We will have the high ground. Ready your weapons, and we go!"

Obi checked on Vestos. He stood ready with his spear. Obi hooked the pot of gruel on the lowest brace on his pack, and unhooked his crossbow. With a bolt loaded, he nodded to Tark.

They yanked open the doors. Outside were a dozen or more ghouls; they seemed surprised by the sudden appearance of their party. Obi felt the heat of the fire at his back and could smell the ghouls' breath on his face, the unmistakable stench of decay and rotting meat.

For a moment, no one moved or dared to breathe, then chaos broke loose. Tug jumped out the door, without his usual war cry.

The ghouls were not so quiet. Their moans went to shrill screams and high-pitched shrieks, so loud that Obi's ears rang. The ghouls charged forward to meet them.

Obi aimed to the right and fired at the nearest ghoul. The bolt went through the throat of the first ghoul and lodged in the eye of a second, and they both went down—lucky shots.

Tannon was hurling arrows, but what marks they made Obi didn't know. Tannon yelled at his sister, but Obi couldn't make out what he was saying.

The ghouls closed in, screeching; their intent was clear. They were calling for blood and raising an alarm. They had found their next meal.

Obi could hear a distant shriek of more ghouls being called in. Two pale, thin ghouls lunged forward, hissing. He could feel their cold breath and the smell of rancid meat. Obi wished he could run away, wished he would have stayed at the monastery. He wished to be anywhere but here. Summoning his courage, he charged forward, meeting them at the threshold of the church.

The first one Obi clubbed with his crossbow; the second he stepped up and kicked in the chest hard enough to knock it on its back. The first was back at him, clawing and snarling. Obi warded off the claws with the crossbow but could do nothing to beat back the unnaturally strong monster. Obi's footing was giving way. The ghoul was thin, wiry, and strong. Obi pressed the crossbow against it, warding off its sharp claws. The black mouth was snapping its triangular teeth at him; the ghoul was stronger than Obi. He was going down under the fangs of the creature. His nightmare was coming true. He wanted to call out, but everyone was already outside the church. It was too late; he would fall, and the ghouls would eat him.

A flash of movement appeared under his arm. Vestos's spear came between Obi and the ghoul and pierced its foul heart. Obi kicked the ghoul off his spear and clubbed another ghoul to his right, shattering his crossbow. He used the momentum of his blow to spin and aim a back kick to another ghoul to his left. Obi was in the fight for his life.

He spun to see how his friends were faring; his heart sank. Layna was down beneath the claws of a ghoul; Tannon was rushing to her aid. Tark and Delvar were surrounded, and Tug was pressed up against the church wall, barely fending off two more. Vestos abandoned the church, as the burning roof began to collapse, and was jabbing at two ghouls himself. Obi's kick had knocked his ghoul back, but two more had joined the fray. Facing three ghouls himself, it was senseless for his companions to die this way and so very unfair; rage replaced his fear. Using his newfound anger, Obi charged the ghouls, intent on taking them into death's embrace. He threw the remains of his crossbow at the one on his left, kicked the one to his right, and blocked the talons of the last, smashing his elbow into the creature's head. Heedless of its fangs, Obi stuck again with his elbow, breaking teeth and bone.

The roof caved in, collapsing, sending a wave of blistering heat out the church door and windows. The ghouls were thrown back, as everyone was splashed with heat and embers. Obi grabbed the ghoul with broken teeth by the hair and chin. He twisted hard, breaking its neck. It fell away.

Obi looked for the next threat. To his surprise the ghouls were running to the shadows of the forest. Obi knew now that they don't fear fire but the sun. The first rays of the sun had come up. The warm life-giving light was more than the ghouls could stand. Obi stood panting, overwhelmed by the excitement and fear of the battle. He could hardly believe the quick turn of events.

Layna let out a sigh. Turning toward the sound, Obi saw Tannon cradling Layna in his arms and feared the worst. Obi rushed to their side to see what aid he could give. "Where are you hurt?"

Layna's pained smile came first. Then she said, "Oh, I feel silly. I turned my ankle on a stone, trying to duck a ghoul. I'll be fine."

Tannon fretted. "You could have died! You are only alive now because those things cannot stand the light of day."

She waved him off. "Yes, but I do live, so help me up."

Obi looked around to see how the others were doing. To his relief all were alive, but now they were a ragged-looking bunch. Tug was limping away from the heat of the church, and he was joined by Vestos leaning heavily on his spear's haft. Tark was bleeding from a head wound. Delvar was sweating and examining a hole in his cloak that seemed to greatly irritate him. Tannon seemed to be fine, as he carefully tended to his sister. Obi himself felt so very tired and became aware of a sharp pain in his arm.

Tark cleared his throat. "Come! Let's get the hell away from this place."

"Just a minute," Tannon snapped. "Layna can hardly move."

Tark, still battle-ready, turned to face Tannon.

Vestos's calm low voice stopped an argument before it began. "Easy, gentlemen. Let's tend our wounds for a moment and then go. Now is not the time to fight each other."

Tug was not in the mood to be attended to and snapped, "I'm fine, just tired!"

Obi could tell Tug was lying by the way he was hunched over, so Obi checked Tark, who was dabbing his temple.

Delvar came through the battle without injury. "Take heart. The scar will not be visible, and you will have a fine tale to tell the barmaids."

"All of us will have a tale to tell," Tark said.

Delvar continued, "Obi, it is a testament to your good nature that you wish to help your comrades who are wounded, but you should really tend to yourself now."

Obi looked down at his sleeve, with the dark ghoul blood mixed with his. It was a small cut that caused his arm to ache. Carefully he pulled back his sleeve and revealed the deep gashes on each side of his elbow. He wiped away some of the blood with the corner of his sleeve. The cuts were ragged but not as deep as they had first appeared. There was little he could do. Already Obi's arm stiffened some. "It looks worse than it is."

The party gathered around Layna and Tannon. He had used his scarf to bind up Layna's ankle, but she was still having trouble putting weight on the foot.

Obi said, "We should have some breakfast, while I find a branch that you can use for a crutch."

The party turned and stared at Obi like he was a fool.

Tug growled out, "And what would you have us eat?"

Obi pulled out the cauldron and water skin. "Vestos's morning porridge and tea of course!"

Surprised, Vestos laughed loudly; the others laughed too.

"Through all this, you held on to our breakfast?" Vestos wiped a tear from his eye. "Obi, you are a pearl among men!"

His ears turned red with embarrassment. Obi stammered out, "I couldn't leave the porridge behind. It would be wasteful."

Delvar clapped Obi across the back. "Right. Obi, you are indeed a good man to have around! Let's find a crutch for Layna and eat and be gone. I do not wish to be on this side of the wall for another night!"

There were hearty agreements all around. Obi took a swig of the herbal tea and then excused himself to search for a suitable crutch. The ghouls could not be far, and there was no way Obi was going to venture into the shadows alone. Fortunately he found a stick nearly as tall as he was that could be cut down to a suitable size. It even had a smaller pair of branches that split apart, forming a notch for Layna's arm. By the time Delvar had shaped the crutch, everyone had eaten breakfast and had drunk the last of the tea.

Seventeen

We need to make it back before sunset.

The morning sun was warm, and it seemed like they would easily survive their adventure. They were making good time considering all but much slower than they had when coming here. Tug and Vestos looked bad. Although they didn't say anything, Obi noticed Tug had kept from facing the sun.

Obi worried, however, that they were not moving very fast, and they still had the river to cross and a long, hard rope climb. No one had thought about what they would do if they were wounded and unable to climb the rope. Obi had been more worried about the rope being discovered and cut than climbing it.

Tannon helped Layna along with her crutch. Obi assisted Vestos. Delvar offered a shoulder to Tug, who waved him off. The party headed back to the Dragonwall.

The walk was taking its toll on Tug and Vestos. Obi noticed that Tug had accepted Delvar's offer to help some time ago.

By midmorning, they stopped under the shade of some tall bushes. Obi dropped his pack and propped Vestos against it. He made his way to Tark. "I am going to scout around for water. Vestos and Tug could really use some."

"I think we all could. Don't go too far though. We have to keep moving. We still have to cross the river and, as it looks, haul a couple of us up that damn wall."

Obi nodded and turned away. He wasn't the only one who was worried. Obi jogged in a wide circle around the parties' resting spot but didn't find any water.

When he got back to Vestos, he looked even more tired than when Obi left.

"Obi, don't exhaust yourself. We still have a long way to go."

Vestos knows we are in trouble, Obi thought. "All right."

Vestos continued, "We will get a drink at the river. Tug and I will be fine till then."

Obi tried to tease Vestos. "What about me? I get very thirsty."

He grinned. "Oh, don't whine. It's not becoming of a librarian."

Obi helped Vestos to his feet. Together they hobbled after Delvar and Tug.

The morning grew warmer, and their pace slowed. They were all beginning to suffer from dehydration. When they stopped for a longer rest around noon, Obi went to Tark. This time Delvar followed him.

Obi examined the wound at Tark's forehead; it was raised and red. "Tark, I think these stops should be shorter. Vestos is growing weaker. I don't know how long before I will be carrying him."

Tired and grouchy, Tark snapped, "I know. I can see that."

Delvar eased in close; his sly look made Obi sense something was wrong but was too tired to care. "I am going to scout for water."

"I will look too." Tark pointed to the west. "You go that way, and I will look this way."

Delvar raised a hand. "Maybe we should go on ahead and make sure the rope is secure and then bring water back for the others."

A feeling of dread filled Obi. It wasn't what Delvar was saying, but the way he had mentioned it. He was suggesting that they leave the wounded behind. Obi knew Delvar was a survivor but at the expense of their friends? Obi would not have thought it possible.

Tark grew quiet. He spoke slowly. His words were calm, but anger was in his eyes. "We are not leaving the others."

"We could come back for them." In a confident and soothing tone, Delvar said, "I am sure some water would perk everyone up, and it would be nice to know that the rope is safe."

STROM & MONTOYA

Tark's hand dropped to the hilt of his sword. He spoke through gritted teeth. "And I suppose you would be willing to stay behind and guard the rope, just so it would be there when we got back."

Delvar rolled his hand across his mustache. "Ah, well, I hadn't thought of that. But now that you mention it—"

Tark cut him off. "You are free to do as you please. What about you, Obi?"

Obi had thought of leaving the group the day before, when everyone was healthy and strong, but not now with half the party wounded. Obi had made a promise to Tark, to his Sovereign. "I won't leave the party."

Delvar smiled. "I wasn't suggesting just leaving them. I just thought of the greater good, bringing back water and ensuring the rope was safe. That's all."

"Let me know how the swim is," Tark snapped. "Oh, that's right. You don't swim." He turned away and went looking for water.

Delvar raised his hands contritely. "Obi, I wasn't saying we abandon our friends."

Obi was shaken by Delvar's approach to their situation. "We need to stick together."

Delvar's tone softened. "We need to remember that the rope may be found. It is for the good of all of us to make sure the rope is safe, so we all are safe. Then we would come back and help them. Get water for Vestos and Tug. Make sure Layna and Tannon are fine."

Obi thought for a moment. Delvar's words were comforting and soothing. "You make good points, Delvar."

Delvar gave him a comforting grin. "Good man, we can set off immediately."

"You misunderstand me. I can't leave my friends." Obi didn't wait for an answer. He took off at a jog.

Delvar's smile faded; his thick arms flexed, as he rolled his hand across his mustache. Delvar called out, "Obi, wait! Let me explain."

Obi didn't want to hear the soft words or the easy choice of leaving behind his friends. He had thought along the same lines—before the church, when everyone was fine. But now he would not leave anyone injured. Delvar's voice grew distant. Obi kept his pace and rolled along, skirting the tree line, not wanting to catch site of any ghouls. He wondered if Delvar would take off on his own to find the rope. Obi jogged along, taking moderate strides, but his legs were getting heavy, and his whole arm ached. He wondered how bad Vestos and Tug were feeling. He made his way in a large circle. Alongside a clump of bushes sat a moderate-size mud puddle. It wasn't a stream or river, but at least it was water. He ran to it.

His heart sank. The odd-shaped mud puddle had five points, looking like a large hand with thick fingers. Half smashed into the bottom lay the muck of a putrefied ghoul's body. Its pale skin glistened at the bottom, and its head was smashed open with gray and black ichor spilled out. A green sludge floated along the bottom of the pool. Even with the ghoul, Obi thought the water still might be drinkable. He got close. The stench of rotting meat assaulted his nose. He cursed the foul water.

Disappointed, Obi stood up and took off at a jog to finish his survey. He made his way along the tree line, stopping at times to listen for a stream; he heard none. He made his way along a small ridge, before circling back to the clump of shrubs and his party. Vestos lay sleeping on his pack; Tug lay prone. Layna and Tannon stood off a ways chatting.

Obi wondered if Delvar had run off. Obi dismissed the idea.

Tark raised a hopeful glance. Obi knew what Tark meant; he wondered if Obi had found any water. He shook his head. "I found something worse."

Tark raised an eyebrow. "I found old wolf tracks about a week old. What did you find?"

"I found a mud puddle, but a dead ghoul was in it. The whole thing was poisoned by its rotting carcass."

Tark gasped. "A ghoul is out here? It's daylight! How did it die?"

Obi shrugged. "It was dead, sort of smashed. I didn't see any others."

"Bloody hell, Obi. We have traveled a long ways. I thought we had left those things back at the church. We should get moving, short breaks from now on. Move as fast as we can to the river."

Obi agreed with the plan. He just wanted to be on the other side of the wall. He didn't want to fight or run. He just wanted to eat and sleep. His growling stomach reminded him that breakfast was a long time ago.

Tark cleared his throat and clapped. "All right, ready or not, we have to go."

Obi shook Vestos. "We're going to make it to the Dragonwall by nightfall.

Vestos groaned, rolled open an eye, and sat up. "I'm feeling like Tug looks, like dung."

Obi grinned at him, swung up his pack, and helped Vestos to his feet.

Tug snorted and stood up. "Delvar? Where the hell is he? Took a nap under a tree, eh?"

Tark grabbed Tug by the shoulder. "I guess we will let him catch up."

Delvar walked out from the taller shrub. "Just taking the time to smell the roses and fresh air. I circled around and didn't find any water."

Obi was surprised to see him, and, by Tark's expression, he was too.

Tannon took Layna by the arm. "Are you all right?"

She used the crutch to stand. "Of course. It is just a little sprain, a silly thing. It's just my dumb luck to do this."

Delvar took up Tug's other side. Obi had Vestos, and Tannon had Layna. Tark set the pace. Obi and Vestos were quickly passed. Obi was glad to see Delvar sticking with the party. It was the only right thing to do, especially now that half the party was wounded.

They made their way up to the top of the hill and started down the other side. Going through the battlefield was easy enough. The white bones scattered about, as before, served as curiosities, but now, everywhere Obi looked, the white bones looked like grave markers of a large battle. He just hoped that their own bones would not be joining them.

The sun had peaked, and the party was still a long ways off from the river. They had three more short breaks, each one only sapping their energy. Vestos had the idea to just keep walking. "At our pace they would catch us soon enough."

Looking at Tug and Delvar, Obi wondered how Tug could keep walking. He guessed it was sheer will or orneriness. Tension remained between Delvar and Tark. They didn't speak, just kept glaring at the other. Tannon said nothing, save small bits of encouragement to Layna.

The only one who said anything was Layna. She chatted away about growing up, training Swiftwing, and the importance of getting rest. She went on to tell of her childhood and the stories that her father had told growing up. She talked and talked, until Obi thought she would lose her voice. She would clear her throat and start another story.

The party topped a hill, where it flattened out and the valley could be seen. In the distance, Obi could see the line of the Dragonwall illuminated by the afternoon sun. He tried to focus on getting to the river as quickly as Vestos could. Everyone seemed to be of the same mind. Vestos quickened his pace, till they were nearly at a fast walk. They came to the last draw, before descending to the river's edge. Delvar stopped. "About a half a mile to the river."

Hanging heavily onto Delvar's arm, sucking air between each word, Tug gasped out, "A moment's rest."

Tannon had sweat streaking down his face, etched in worry. "We should keep moving. The river is right there."

Tark helped Tug to a nearby boulder. "What are you looking at, Delvar?"

Delvar was bent at the waist and said, "Wolf tracks and a lot of them. By the look of them, about a day old. They might have been following us to the church."

Tannon checked Layna's splint, ensuring the leather bits were fastened and tight. Obi suspected Vestos and Tug were close to exhaustion. He hoped they were able to cross the river. Obi asked nervously, "Delvar, what else did you see?"

Delvar shook his head; he had recovered a bit. "Nothing, but the river is a danger. If there is something here that intends us harm, the river is the place to attack."

Tark let out a loud gasp, trying to catch his breath. "He is right. If I were hunting us, I would run you to the river and make you choose to face my blade or drown."

"So what do we do?" Tannon asked.

Delvar dabbed the sweat from his face with a silk handkerchief he had produced. "Catch our breath for a moment. Look to the path ahead and see places of ambush. We can approach the river with caution and reasonable haste, but we would need to rest before trying to cross anyway."

Tannon nodded agreement. "I'm glad you think of these things, Delvar."

Layna stood up, steadying herself with her crutch. "The raft isn't where we left it. It's gone!"

Although it was hardly a raft, the two logs they had lashed together had made the crossing much easier for everyone. Without a raft, the crossing would be impossible for Vestos and Delvar and probably Tug, who could hardly walk, let alone swim. Obi cried out, "How could it be gone? We pulled it up on the bank. There is no way it could have floated away."

Tannon replied, "I don't know, but I don't see it either."

"Well, I don't see anything waiting to jump out at us, and, if we have to make a new raft, we had better get down there." Delvar too was motivated to get to the river.

Tark cautioned, "Not to be difficult, but isn't this just the kind of distraction that an ambusher would want?"

The group collectively turned and stared at Tark. He continued, "I mean, a moment ago, we were being cautious. Now we are ready run headlong down to the river. That is what I would want you to do."

There was a moment of silence, and then Tannon spoke up. "We cannot second-guess ourselves now. We have to get to the river, and we have to cross it. We are wasting time we do not have. Let's get down there, with caution, find our raft or make a new one, and get the hell out of here!"

There was no arguing with his logic. Everyone got up and started down the hill. Tark drew his sword. Soon they were at the river's edge. The raft was gone. Tark scratched his head. "Are you sure this is where we landed? This doesn't look real familiar."

Delvar lost his wordiness. "Everybody! Look along the shore for something we can make a raft out of."

Tannon went upstream. Obi headed downstream. Obi moved across the rocks, noticing a tree not far from the river that they could cut down. It was big enough for the party to use, like the other one. Obi ran down. There, sitting near the outcropping of rocks, where they had sunned themselves earlier the day before, was the raft. He waved his arms overhead and then cupped his hands to his mouth. "Found it!"

Delvar shouted to Tannon upstream. "We found the raft!"

Layna, still hopeful, said, "Maybe we need only get to the other side of the river."

Delvar continued, "There it is! This looks like where we came out of the water. In the excitement, I didn't realize we had floated down this far."

Obi filled the water skin and shared it with Vestos and Tug. Vestos drank heavily. Panting and coughing, he finished it off. Obi refilled it and his own water skin; everyone did.

Layna stepped into the water. "Oh, my! That water is cold but feels good on my ankle!"

Tark sat on a log. "We are running low on sunlight. Let's go."

Tannon grabbed the side of the raft and heaved. It didn't move. Tark grabbed the other side, then Delvar and Obi. Tug leaned down on one knee, panting. "This raft is damn heavy."

Obi was exhausted; everyone was. They had been up for so long, with little rest and almost no food. He wanted to say something to make it better or to take a positive spin. He said, "It will be good to get over the Dragonwall."

Tug smiled at him. "Damn right!"

Tark counted. They heaved again. The raft slid slowly into the water's edge. A second heave and it was afloat.

Tark threw his pack on the raft, and Obi lashed them down to ensure nothing would be lost.

Delvar looked nervous about getting into the water. "Don't recall it being this damn cold, as cold as that golden light at the church. That was a hell of a trap!"

Tark shot him a stern look. "Now why do you have to bring up that hellish thing?"

Vestos and Tug lay on the middle of the raft, and Obi was quick to loop a piece of rope around each, making sure everyone was secure. Once they were ready, Tannon pushed them from shore.

Obi thought the water was colder now than before. A mist was gathering along the shores of the river, adding to the sense of dread building in him.

The sun was setting, casting long shadows across the Dragonwall. With the cold water and the added exhaustion, the party was at the mercy of the river's current. As they crossed the midpoint of the river, he knew what was bothering him. The Dragonwall reflected the colors of the beautiful sunset, changing the stark white to oranges and reds. Obi thought the wall was beautiful but somehow wrong. The beautiful colors of the Dragonwall reminded him of the ghoul church, before it turned bloodred.

Eighteen
What does that note say?

By the time they dragged themselves ashore, the sun had set. A ground fog was thickening, and the air temperature had cooled. Tark grabbed the lashing of the raft and pulled one end to shore; the other end slid downriver. "We have floated a long ways past the rope, and it is going to take us a while to get back there."

Tannon pushed the raft inland. "Bet me! I will find that rope and will get my sister safely over that blasted Dragonwall."

Obi had no doubt of Tannon's intent and was certain that Tannon would die before giving up on his sister. The cold water had soothed their fever and had quenched their thirst but had given them a case of the shivers. Their hands and feet shook with chills. Vestos had the same look as Tug, with dark circles under his eyes. His lips were bluish, and his fingernails had turned black. The feeling of dread returned, the same feeling as back at the church. Obi concluded that Tug and Vestos were turning into ghouls. He was tempted to blurt out his conclusion but worried, what if he were wrong? For now he would keep his observations to himself.

Layna was walking better. "The river must have healing properties. My ankle is much better. I'm okay, Tannon. Go help Delvar with Tug."

Tannon waited to see how Layna walked before he left her side.

Tark moved to Tug's side. "I will help, Delvar. Let's get going."

Obi guessed it was Tark's way of keeping an eye on Delvar. Since they had crossed the river, there was nothing stopping Delvar from bolting to the rope. Obi tried to get Vestos to stand. The fever had his hands clenched into fists, shaking violently. "I need some help with Vestos."

Layna pointed. "Tannon, go help him."

In a lyrical ranting, Tannon stiffly moved to the other side of Vestos and hoisted him up. Although Obi didn't understand the language, the tone made it clear that Tannon was pissed off with the whole situation and probably worried about his sister more than anything. Obi was quick to catch the other side of Vestos.

Tark and Delvar took hold of Tug, hoisting him to his feet. Tug mumbled through his chills, "Get your hands off me."

Tark patted him. "Don't worry. We have you. You're safe."

The party headed slowly back along the wall dodging sharp rocks, scrub brush with thorns, and ground cactus, each taking turns scraping their legs. A layer of driftwood lay scattered along their path. Tark and Delvar led the group up a small rise closer to the hill. "We could camp here for the night and climb the rope in the morning. The higher ground makes it more defensible."

Tannon blurted out, "No, we find the rope, and we get out!"

Obi knew Tark was just looking out for the party's best interests, trying to keep them safe. A fire would take the chill off Vestos and Tug, but Obi would prefer that fire be on the other side of the Dragonwall. Obi adjusted his grip on Vestos and struggled to keep up with Tannon's pace.

It wasn't long before sweat was beading along Obi's brow. His elbow had been numb during the swim and was now waking up. In the last few paces his arm felt like it was on fire. He bit his lip and readjusted his grip on Vestos. He could hear Layna occasionally wincing behind him. Whatever the cold water had healed, it was wearing off.

They walked along in a quiet, tension-filled march. Obi was happy when Tark called for a halt.

Tannon asked, "Why are we stopping?"

Tark and Delvar sat Tug down on old large deadfall. "I don't see the rope, but we are close."

Tannon sat Vestos down and moved to his sister's side. "Layna, you're hurt?"

Layna pushed him off. "Silly, I'm just giving that ankle a workout."

Obi didn't believe her and doubted if Tannon did either. Swiftwing circled up and landed beside her.

Tark panted out, "Tannon, Obi, scout about. See if you can find the rope. No sense in packing these men any farther than we have to."

Delvar looked like he was going to say something, when Tark cut him off. "Delvar and I will stand guard, in case any ghouls approach."

Obi felt a cold chill more than his wet robes. He had hoped they had left the ghouls across the river. He didn't like the idea of creeping around in the dark when ghouls could be out there. Obi propped up Vestos with his pack. "I'll be right back."

Vestos nodded weakly.

Obi stood up and shook out his arm, flinching at the pain. "Tannon, you head upriver. I'll head downriver along the wall."

Tannon didn't move from his sister's side.

Layna patted him on his arm. "Go, Tannon. The quicker you find the rope, the quicker all of us will get out of here."

Obi didn't need to see Tannon's expression to tell that he was irritated. Obi headed along the wall. The darkness parted slightly, as the moon emerged from the clouds. A low mist was forming along the riverbank. He jogged along, trying to avoid loose rocks, branches, and thorny bushes. He was certain that the wall had been shorter and the ground more steep where they had come over the wall. He ran farther along, until he became certain the rope was not this way.

The river was closer to the wall here, and he was back where they had landed. The mist was coming in, creeping upward, toward the wall. It reminded him of the ghoul's skin color and how pale Vestos and Tug were getting. Over the soft whoosh of the water, he thought he heard something. He realized, in his haste to find the rope, he had forgotten to take a weapon.

He turned around and headed back. Not looking back, he broke into a run. His legs were exhausted; his arm ached, and he was hungry. All those things didn't matter. He sped along toward his party, forcing his feet to go faster. He ran till his lungs burned; he ran till the ground rose up. It was where Tark had said it was defensible. Obi stopped, turned, and peered into the darkness, to see if anything was chasing him. He saw nothing but mist. The feeling of something watching him didn't fade. He broke into a run again, sped along the brush, leaping over small bushes. He slipped on a rolling rock, catching his footing before he fell. He ran back to the party.

Tark sounded irritated. "What the hell? You're making an awful racket! Is there something chasing you?"

Obi slowed to a jog and stopped. A little embarrassed, he said, "No, I got scared. I thought something was coming out of the water. I wasn't going to let it eat me!"

Tark huffed out, "Did you find the rope?"

Obi shook his head, still breathing hard. "No. It is not that way. Tannon might have."

Tannon walked out of the shadows. "I found it."

Tark let out a sigh of relief. "Finally! Let's go!"

Tannon shook his head; his voice cracked as he spoke. "I found a note and the rope. The rope has been cut. The note is for you, Tark."

Tark took a step back, visibly shaken. "The rope is cut?"

Tannon handed the note to him.

Tark read the note, then crumpled and dropped it.

Obi could see it wasn't good news. "What does note say?"

Tark took two steps and sat down hard on the rocks, as if his legs had finally given out.

Obi reached out and picked up the note. In the moonlight the parchment was hard to read; he held it up and read it out loud:

Tark, the dragon hunter,
Crossing the Dragonwall is a one-way trip.
Captain Samuel Jacobs

Feelings of dread swelled in Obi. The only haven they had found in this retched place was the church, and they had burned it down. The way out was cut off, and the sun had set. The undead would be on their party soon. Frustration, confusion, and sadness gripped him. "We are all going to die, torn apart by ghouls."

Nineteen

You had better move it.

Their only means of escape from this retched place was the rope, and it was cut, lying in a large coil. Obi wished he had never left the monastery and had never heard about the Dragonwall. Frustration, fear, and sadness formed a tight knot in the pit of his stomach. "We are all going to die."

His friends fell silent, except Tug, who let out a raspy laugh. "I knew that prick Jacobs was trouble."

They needed a way out. Obi's mind spun. They needed direction. "Tark! What are we going to do? How are we going to fix this? What's the plan?"

Tark yanked his sword, pointing it high over his head. He kicked over a piece of drift wood and swung his blade, hacking at the air. He kicked rocks, stomped the ground, yelling curses. He took a deep breath and sat down. Quietly he said, "You were right, Tannon. We should have gotten a permit."

Obi was afraid to ask again but, unwilling to wait, did again. "How do we fix this? How do we get over the wall?"

Tark threw up his hands. "Hell, Obi, I don't know. We need some ideas."

Obi shook his hands in a nervous motion. "Tannon, could you use your grappling hook?"

Tannon let out a huff. "I have never thrown it that high, and, in the dark, who knows if it would catch on anything. I suppose I could try."

Tannon moved to the wall. He whipped the grappling hook around in a large circle before sending it skyward. It caught nothing and fell back. He tried several more times before returning. "It is too high."

Obi blurted out, "Delvar's very strong, and he could try."

Delvar waved a hand. "Calm down, Obi. I don't have the skill that Tannon has. We are not going to make it over the wall tonight. We have to split up. If we each head out and look around, maybe we can find an easier way up or a place to hide."

Tannon stood up. "That's crazy! You just want to leave, because you think you have a better chance alone, while the ghouls eat the rest of us."

Delvar snarled back, "I'm trying to save my ass and yours too! We haven't seen anything on this side of the river that is of any danger to us. We need to spread out and find a place to hold up for the night."

Tannon shouted back, "Is that so? What about Tug and Vestos? How will they fare, if we split up, or were you going to take one of them with you?"

Delvar jabbed his thumb into his chest. "I intend to get through this one way or another! I am looking out for everyone, not just my precious sister!"

"Is that why you wanted to leave everyone this afternoon? To get water and secure the rope, or was it to save your ass?" Tannon yelled; his words stung the air.

Obi could see the disagreement was becoming heated with a growing fierceness. He raised his hands and stepped between the angry men. Obi apologized, "I didn't mean to start an argument."

Delvar ignored Obi and fumed. "All Tannon does is whine about what we are doing or not doing, and then the mother-hen act with his sister. I'm sick of it!"

"At least I care about someone other than myself, you posturing peacock!"

"Tannon, really," Layna scolded.

Tark shouted, "ENOUGH! You two shut your mouth."

Delvar rolled back on his heels, throwing open his arms. "Frick that! I knew I should have run for the rope when I had the chance! Damn it! Damn you, Tark!"

Tark stood slouched in front of Delvar, while his hand slipped to the pommel of his longsword. "What, Delvar? You were going to abandon us?"

Delvar took a step closer, dwarfing Tark by a head, pointing a finger at his face. "I have a good mind to thrash you right here."

Layna tried to diffuse the argument. "We could go to the river, get on the raft, and stay there."

Tannon shook his head. "And die in that forsaken river? No thank you. The hill is sounding better, at least it is defensible."

Tark turned his attention to Layna. "That is a good plan, but we will keep that as a backup."

Delvar shook his fist. "Still giving orders, Tark?"

Tark rolled back to face Delvar. "We are not done for yet. We still have fight enough in us to take a stand. We have metal in our hands and fire in our bellies."

Delvar waved a large fist in Tark's face. "You are so full of yourself! This is shit! Obi is right. We are going to die here, this night."

Tark's mood darkened. "No! We're not. We'll make it back to that damn rise and wait till morning, then we travel back. About a week to the next town, then we get out."

Delvar threw up his hands, pointing to Vestos and Tug. "Those two are changing into ghouls, if you haven't noticed their freaky nails and dark circles around their eyes. They have till dawn, maybe, before they change. And your wound is infected too. We won't make it through tonight let alone one or two weeks."

Obi's elbow ached. He wondered if he was infected and how long before he changed to a ghoul. He wondered if he would have to kill Vestos, once he fully changed into a ghoul.

Delvar leaned into Tark. "They build this wall to keep things out, to keep us out!"

Tark looked pissed off, matching Delvar's mood. "I know that! Tell me something that is helpful!"

Layna hushed him. Her gaze fixed, she pointed off into the darkness and whispered, "Something is moving out there. I can't make out what it is, but it's quick."

Obi looked but saw nothing. The moon had made its way into the sky, casting a glow across the valley, revealing the growing layer of wispy fog quickly enveloping the land.

Delvar and Tark stopped midargument, frozen, staring into the darkness.

A movement in the growing mist caught Obi's attention. Fifty paces into the darkness, something made the mist swirl with small streaks, like ripples on a pond.

Layna whispered, "There it is! Did you see it?"

The movements made chills run across Obi's back. "I saw it."

Motioning for everyone to follow, Tark whispered, "We are going to the rise."

Tark glared at Delvar and Tannon. "No arguments. This is what we are going to do."

"Why …" Delvar started.

Tark continued. "Shut up, Delvar. Tannon, go gather up the rope that you found. We are going to need it. Obi, help Layna. I got Tug. Delvar you take Vestos. We are going back to that little rise where we saw the deadfall up against the wall. It's defensible, and there is a supply of firewood. We will build fires and hold off anything that might show up. We know the ghouls are afraid of fire. Most other things are too."

Delvar still fumed. "Why the hell should we do it your way? Following you got us into this mess!"

Tark walked up to Delvar and looked him in the eye. "We're going to do this my way, because it's a better plan than listening to your blustering. If you don't like it, you are free to leave and hide in darkest hole you can find. In the meantime you had better move it, or you are the one who will be left behind."

Delvar looked menacingly in the dark. "It was deer out there, nothing more."

Tark ignored him and turned away. "Tannon, go! Meet us at the rise."

Obi went over to Layna and Tannon. "Come on, Tannon, please. I've got Layna." Obi feared that Tannon would refuse, that the party was going to come apart right then. Tannon clenched his jaw and stood firm. Layna spoke to him in their singsong elvish way.

Tannon snarled and turned away, running into the night. Obi put his arm around Layna's small frame. She was much lighter than Vestos and smelled better. "Is Tannon coming back?"

Patting him softly across his back, Layna said, "Of course. He knows this is the best plan."

In a slow, methodical pace, they moved along the wall. Tannon, with a large coil of rope over one shoulder, caught up with them before they managed to get to the deadfall. Tannon took Layna's arm. "I have her."

Obi could see Tannon was still angry, but his ire was not directed at Obi. He hurried ahead to catch up with Tark. He took Tug's free arm and threw it over his shoulder.

Tark gave a surprised glance at Obi before shifting Tug's weight between them and dragging him along.

It seemed to take forever to get up the slight hill where they had passed the fallen trees. The moon had risen, but it could hardly be seen, making little more than a dim glow through haze. Obi realized that it was a bit of luck that they had found the rise. If they had they waited longer, the mist would have been too thick to find anything at all.

Two large trees had fallen over with their tops resting against the Dragonwall, forming a V-shaped fence on each side of the hill. The Dragonwall to their backs and the trees down on each side, there was only a small opening for anything to approach their group.

Tark and Obi dropped the unconscious Tug to the ground in the center of the camp. Delvar eased Vestos down onto a nearby boulder. Tannon and Layna sat with their backs against the wall itself. Swiftwing appeared out of the mist and landed on the uprooted stump of one of the trees.

Vestos sat up; his head wobbled back and forth. In a hoarse voice, he said, "Well, we made it here. That's a good sign."

"Hopefully we have nothing to worry about being this close to the wall," Layna added.

Delvar smirked. "Perhaps."

Tark asked, "Obi, do you have the strength to get materials for a fire?"

Obi was too tired, too cold, and too hungry to gather anything. He wasn't sure, but he hoped he had the strength. He knew he had to. He was the only one who could. "Yes, of course."

Tark pointed at the very top of the rise, where Tug lay. "Delvar, make a fire pit here. Tannon, Obi, and I will get more wood."

Delvar's tone was surly. "I don't think a fire is a good idea. It will be a beacon for anything around to be drawn right to us."

Tark let out a heavy sigh. "You're right, Delvar, but I don't think we have a choice. We get caught in the dark, and we will be in bigger trouble."

Delvar mocked, "Because we haven't looked for shelter."

Ignoring Delvar, Tark continued. "We are going to need a fire to survive the cold night."

Tannon stood up, looking Delvar in the eye. "I'll get the fire pit ready. You can gather firewood and look for a dark hole to hide in while you're at it."

Delvar snapped back, "Think what you will, but it's good to consider all our options." With a swirl of his cloak, Delvar turned away and disappeared into the darkness.

Tark shrugged. "He will be back, but he is free to go his own way. I will tell you this. If he leaves and gets into trouble, I won't risk everyone to save him."

The mist had grown thicker, and it was hard to see very far in the dim moonlight. Fortunately they did not have to go far from camp to get driftwood.

Tark picked up a large limb. "What the hell happened to these trees? Why are they all uprooted and knocked over?"

Obi had been thinking the same thing but had been too tired to voice it. "A rock slide?"

Tark gathered a few more limbs. "A rockslide or an earthquake?"

Some of the trees were uprooted; others were broken off in the thick portions of their trunks. Obi had thought maybe a great wind blew across here. He shrugged; following a trail of large broken limbs, he wrapped them up with his leather cord.

Tark called, "Obi, give me a hand with this tree. I think the two of us could drag it up to the camp."

Obi set down the limbs he had gathered and moved toward Tark's voice. "Where are you?"

"Right here." His voice came from below and to his left.

Obi took a few steps, moving carefully through the loose rocks. Something rushed past him, bushing along the rocks, and quickly away down the hill. A chill ran down Obi's spine; the movement seemed somehow sinister. Cautiously Obi called out, "Tark, Delvar?"

Out of the mist, Tark appeared, holding his fingers to his lips. "Let's grab this tree and get back."

"Did you see it? Something was beside me."

Tark grasped the top of a dead, dry pine tree. "I thought I heard something moving. It could be Delvar, but I don't know. Let's get this tree to our camp."

Obi took hold of the tree across from Tark. Together they had little trouble dragging it along. If he had not been so tired, Obi thought that he could have done it on his own. As it was, he and Tark barely managed to drag the tree back to camp. The tree seemed to protest being dragged, snapping branches and causing several rocks to go tumbling down the hill.

When they neared the camp, Tannon called to them. "Tark, Obi? What are you doing?"

They came out of the mist. Tannon came forward to help, clearly relived that it was his companions making the racket and not something else. Together they dragged the tree into the narrow opening.

Tark stopped. "We can set it here at the base of the tree, where the branches are widest. It will help enclose the camp. See? It nearly blocks the narrow opening of our fence."

Tannon interrupted, "Where is Delvar?"

"Don't know. It is so dark out there. I thought I saw something move in the mist, but I don't know what it was." Tark cursed under his breath and shouted, "Delvar!"

His voice echoed in the darkness. No response.

Obi hoped Delvar would make it back soon. He did not want to think that Delvar would abandon the group in this situation or be reckless enough to go out on his own.

Tark, clearly irritated, said, "Tannon, we can call for Delvar as we get more wood. Obi, you and Layna see about getting a fire going."

Feelings of dread and exhaustion overwhelmed Obi. He hoped whatever it was in the mist was not ghouls. He hoped it was Delvar trying to scare the group, but, deep down, Obi knew whatever it was, it was dangerous, probably more dangerous than the ghouls. Obi tried to keep his voice from cracking. "Be careful. Something is out there."

Tark shrugged. "Obi and I couldn't get a good look at it. I'll gather wood, while you guard my back."

Tannon pulled his bow and strung it. "Like before? The deer or more like ghouls?"

Tark checked his sword. "Don't know. Could be nothing or it could be Delvar messing around. Whatever it is, I don't want to take chances. Obi, get the fire going. We won't be long."

Obi stammered back, "I am not sure this is a good idea. I can hardly see anything."

"It's the only idea I have," Tark said.

Tannon nodded and followed Tark through the opening in the fallen trees. Obi snapped off a few small branches from the dead pine tree that they had just dragged in, and took them over to Layna and the fire pit that Tannon had constructed. Obi hurried to the nearest tree and broke off the largest branches he could manage, and gathered tree moss too, hoping it would make good kindling.

Some distance away, Tark and Tannon were calling for Delvar, as before. Obi didn't hear Delvar calling back.

Layna took the branches and began stripping off the needles, gathering a pile of small tinder. Tug was snoring fitfully on the ground nearby, and Vestos now sat on the ground, leaned up against the rock. It appeared to Obi that his friend was on the verge of passing out.

Obi pulled out his flint and steel, and began striking. Layna scooped the tinder back into a pile. It seemed to him that his world had shrunk to just this little area inside the downed trees.

Tannon and Tark came stumbling out of the darkness, back into camp. Tark dropped a large armload of wood next to the fire pit. "There is something out there, and it's not Delvar." Tark groaned and limped up the hill.

Obi just wanted to be warm and safe. He cursed himself under his breath; his hands were giving him trouble. He struck the flint; the bright flash of the sparks made it hard to see the tinder after the light faded. He couldn't get the spark to land on the tinder.

Layna laid a gentle hand on his shoulder; she moved closer, and gathered a handful of dry moss and twigs. "Slow down, Obi. You'll get it. You always do."

Obi was thankful for Layna's support. He took a deep breath and composed himself and stuck the flint. A hot spark landed on the moss; a small wisp of smoke followed. He dared to breathe one breath across it, trying to nurture it into a glowing ember. A scream shattered the air. Obi jumped, scattering the pile of tinder and putting out the ember. Obi uttered a few curse words.

He and Layna looked down the hill into the darkness. The sound of grunting and running, stumbling feet could be heard. Rocks went rolling down the hill as something approached the camp. Obi scrambled to get to Vestos's spear. Layna drew one of her sickles and called out, "Tannon!"

Tark and Tannon came tearing into the camp. Tark held a club in one hand and his sword in the other. "OBI! We need that fire!"

Tannon came close behind, looking over his shoulder as he stumbled along.

Tark turned away, throwing down the club, and pulled the tree around to close the opening.

Obi turned back to the fire pit. "What did you see?"

Tark panted. "Didn't see anything. I heard that bloodcurdling scream, and a bunch of crashing and thrashing around just down the hill."

Layna asked, "Did you see Delvar?"

Tark shook his head. Tannon ran up behind Obi and turned to defend the camp with his bow.

Obi gathered up the tinder and felt around for his flint that he had dropped. A hand patted his shoulder. Obi jumped. "Vestos!"

Vestos knelt next to him; his lips had turned a ghostly blue, and his eyes were encircled with dark blotches. He spoke in a calm whisper. "Get more wood in the pit. I will start the fire."

Obi paused for a moment and then did as Vestos bade. Obi piled a fair amount of tinder and small sticks into the fire pit.

Vestos waggled a finger at him. "More."

Obi added larger branches, and held out his flint and steel. Vestos waved away the tools and instead thrust his hand into the center of the woodpile. He spoke a few words. Obi didn't understand the words. They seemed like the elvish that Tannon and Layna spoke, but these were different. The air vibrated with each syllable. Vestos was channeling magic.

Dim yellow streams of magical energy ran down Vestos's forearm like veins of light and gathered at his hand, growing brighter. With a flash and a pop, his hand and the wood burst into flame.

Obi jumped back. He was amazed at what Vestos had done. "How did you do that?"

Vestos pulled his hand from the fire and smiled. "See? Not even singed."

Obi wanted to hug him, cheer, and thank him for starting the fire. "That was amazing."

Vestos's eyes rolled up into his head, and he passed out, dropping over backward.

Obi hurried to his friend's side; he was burning with fever, but he had this odd little grin. Obi moved Vestos away from the fire and tried to prop him up against the rocks.

Tark called, "Good job, Obi!"

"It wasn't me. It was Vestos. He used magic. But he has passed out, same as Tug."

Tark came over to see for himself. He knelt next to Vestos and cursed. "Damn, I had hoped he could use his magic to get us out of this mess."

"Hadn't we better look for Delvar?"

Tark's head snapped up. "I am not sure that's a good idea. Stoke that fire, so Delvar can see where we are at. Maybe he can find his way to us."

Obi thought of arguing in favor of looking for Delvar, but this was not the time. He nursed the fire into a large blaze. "We barely have enough wood to keep the fire this large. Even if we burned the three trees making our fence, it won't last long."

Layna added more wood pieces, scurrying from this pile to that pile to feed the fire pit.

Obi went to Tark. "We need more wood."

Tark didn't look at Obi but continued to stare out into the dark. "Yeah, you're right."

"I was thinking that I would go get some more and look for Delvar at the same time."

Tark's tone hardened. "That's a bad idea."

Obi tried to figure out how much firewood they needed to burn through the night. "Plus we need to find Delvar, before he gets into real trouble."

Tark countered, shaking his head. "But we don't need to lose another friend."

Obi twisted the argument. "I can gather more timber and look for Delvar."

Tark stared into Obi's eyes. "No. Not alone. We will stay in the light, and we will be quick." Not taking his eyes off Obi, Tark called over his shoulder, "Tannon! Obi and I are going to get more wood. Yell if we go to a point where you can't see us."

Tannon stuck six arrows into the ground before him. "Delvar's not worth the risk."

Tark waved Obi to lead on. "We need the firewood and the friend."

Obi took a step down the hill. Something leaped over the fallen tree behind them. Layna screamed. It crashed into Tark's shoulders and knocked him into Obi, who stumbled forward, landing hard on the rocky shale. A jagged rock cut Obi's face. Pain shot through his cheek; he cried out.

A snarling growl came from behind him.

Tannon let loose an arrow and yelled, "Holy shit!"

Heavy claws dug into Obi's back, tearing through his robes, but leaped away. Obi looked up. A large pale dog jumped over the other tree and disappeared into the night. Tark and Obi scrambled to get up, as Tannon rushed to their side, another arrow nocked.

Tark yelled out, "What the hell was that?"

"I don't know, but it wasn't a ghoul," Tannon yelled.

Obi rubbed his cheek. "Did you hit it?"

"I don't think so. It was too fast," Tannon said.

Obi continued, "We have to get Delvar."

Tark grabbed Obi by arm, pointing beyond the fallen tree. "It's too late. Delvar is lost to us."

Obi stopped, looking where Tark was pointing. Just beyond the edge of the firelight, Obi could see half a dozen pairs of green catlike eyes shining in the darkness.

Twenty
Lost in the black.

Obi stared into the dark swirling mist, trying to see what creatures lurked in the shadows. At the edge of the firelight, a dozen sets of green eyes stared back. When he would stare into them, they would wink out, only to reappear in another place. He could not see what manner of creature the eyes belonged to, but he could see the malice in their eyes. He hoped Delvar was still alive.

Tark shouted, "Layna! Build up that fire!"

The shout startled Obi; he jumped. "What about Delvar?"

Tark ignored his question, shouting over his shoulder, "Obi, arm yourself!"

He wanted to protest, but this wasn't the time. Tark was their leader, and he would keep them safe. Obi's crossbow was broken, and he had no other weapons, except a small dagger in his pack. Tug had a thick short sword, and Vestos had a spear, neither of whom was in any condition to fight with them.

Tark commanded, "Delvar is on his own. We need to protect ourselves. Go!"

Tannon had drawn his bow and was rapidly shifting his aim from one set of eyes to another. Tark drew his sword and backed his way to the fire.

Obi leaped to where Vestos lay. "I need your spear, my friend."

Vestos didn't move; he lay on his back, his face blotchy and pale. His lips had turned blue. He lay unconscious with a slight grin, still pleased about starting the fire.

Obi hefted the spear and took a position on the far side of the fire.

Tark motioned for Obi to move out a little farther, forming a triangle. "We can watch each other's back, and Layna can tend the fire."

Obi noticed how Tark and Tannon had taken up the position without discussion, as if they had rehearsed it many times. Obi surmised their time spent in the militia had honed their battle skills.

Layna began throwing tree limbs on the fire, and, for a moment, the fire dimmed before the new fuel burst into flame. Obi saw the green eyes surge forward as the light lowered. He shouted, "They're coming!"

"I see it!" Tark yelled.

Tannon loosed an arrow into the darkness. A heavy thud followed; the arrow had found its mark. A snarling squeal rang out. The eyes surged forward again.

Tark held his sword with both hands, preparing for the onslaught. "Now we made them mad!"

Feelings of apprehension and fright filled Obi. His heart hammering in his chest, he braced himself for the attack. He gripped Vestos's spear with both hands, planting the shaft onto the ground. If the things were bounding over the deadfalls, he would try to impale them. Even though most of the spear's weight was on the ground, it felt heavy and slow in Obi's hands. How would his group get through the night? Obi dreaded the answer and the thought of dying here; no one at the monastery would ever know.

Tark called out, "Stay close to us, and stay on your feet. Obi, wipe that look off your face. We are not going to die. We are as vicious as they come. We have fire in our bellies and steel in our hands!"

Obi thought Tark was saying those things to himself, as well as the rest of the group, in an attempt to keep up morale. Whatever the reason, it made Obi feel better.

Tark commanded, "Layna, see if you can make some torches."

She didn't respond but began collecting wood that might be torch-worthy.

Obi could see movement to his left and straight in front of him. The savage green eyes did not wink out but narrowed and dropped a few inches, just as cat's eyes would as it readied to pounce. Obi caught his breath to shout.

A guttural war cry tore through the night, nearly causing him to drop the spear in fright. The staring eyes winked out, and the limbs on the fire caught. Obi saw a pale emaciated shape leap back into the shadows.

Obi stole a glance over his shoulder, afraid to look away from the dark. Tark had charged the makeshift barricade as another of the creatures had become entangled in the dead limbs of the fallen tree.

The twang of Tannon's bow sent an arrow hissing into the darkness.

Beyond the barricade out in the darkness, a deep voice was cursing and shouting. Obi recognized it immediately. "Its Delvar!"

Trying to watch his side of the fire and Tark's, Obi turned to see what was happening. He hoped to see for certain that Delvar had returned.

Tark thrust at the creature tearing into the tree. Obi thought it a wolf, but the pale pink limbs were wrong. The thing was dog-shaped, hairless, and terribly thin. It moved on four legs and had a long ratlike tail with weeping sores on the pink folds of its flesh. The body was emaciated but powerful and quick. The head was too large for its body, giving it a rounded look, with a snout shorter and broader than a wolf. Its broad nose and wide mouth were too large for the bright green eyes, making them seem narrow set. The ears were ragged triangles of tattered flesh that stuck up. The mouth was the worst part. It seemed to split the creature's skull from side to side and was filled with many oversize jagged teeth.

Tark stabbed at the wolf but missed. The creature was agile and quick, giving no ground and still avoiding Tark's sword. It pushed through the downed tree, tearing off tree limbs with a strength that belied its starved look.

Tark struck again, and the monster launched forward with an angry snarl. The blow hit Tark in the chest. The claws screeched across his armor and knocked him back.

A loud commotion on the other side of the barricade—breaking tree limbs, rolling rocks, snarls—grew more intense. Obi could not see, but he could hear Delvar cursing and shouting, and then the sound of heavy blows.

Just as suddenly as the green eyes had appeared, they winked out, melting back into the darkness.

Obi looked back at Tark; the monster was gone. The branches torn out were the only signs that it had been here. Tark stood vigilant, staring into the mist.

Delvar staggered into the firelight through the small opening in the barricade, struggling to keep his footing. "Help me close this gap."

Obi grabbed the top of the tree he and Tark had dragged into camp, and together he and Delvar closed the opening.

Layna pushed her way in and threw her arms around Delvar's neck, giving him a big hug.

Tark asked, "Where did you come from?"

Delvar hugged Layna, picking her up off her feet and setting her down at his side. "Right after I left the camp, I saw two of those hairless wolves moving through the mist and then heard another. I would have called a warning but felt, if I followed behind, I might surprise our ambushers."

Tark patted him on the shoulder. "I am surprised to see you alive!"

Being the center of attention, Delvar was clearly pleased and rolled a hand across his mustache and winked at Layna.

"You were saying?" Layna said, waggling a torch at him.

Delvar continued. "I followed them, but they moved too quickly for me. I lost them in the fog. I heard you get attacked and move back to the camp, so I tried to do the same but found the way blocked by more of these diseased wolves. I saw the fire start, so I bided my time and waited. But, as you know, there was not much time to wait. I was able to get closer to camp. When I felt the wolf pack was going in for the kill, I ambushed them, armed with my long sword, and here I am." Delvar grinned broadly.

Tark slapped him across the arm. "It's good to have you here."

Tannon and Layna nodded in agreement. Obi was relieved that Delvar was back. Perhaps they would make it through the night after all.

A howl split the silence, echoing off the Dragonwall, making it difficult to tell its direction. Everyone fell silent, looking into the mist, trying to determine where it was coming from. *Howls are never a good sign*, Obi thought.

In the distance several more howls answered their call. Just beyond the edge of camp, a mournful howl answered. Barking and growls sounded from all sides of camp.

The small group looked at each other in stunned silence. Tark clapped his hands together. "Shit! We are not done yet! Layna build up the fire! The rest of us should see if we can't drag the trees closer to the fire. We need less space to defend and a thicker barricade."

Tark shouted orders. "Tannon, cover us with your bow. Obi, take Tug's short sword and cut down the brush and shrubs around the camp. We can add it to our wall."

Delvar sheathed his sword and grabbed for a tree. Obi grabbed Tug's short sword from his belt and headed to the closest shrub.

Tark asked, "How long do you think we have?"

Layna stopped gathering branches and turned her attention to Tark. "If these creatures are wolves, they will gather their strength and attack, if they think they can win."

"Gods, do you think they are werewolves?" Obi stammered out.

Layna giggled. "No, they seem like rabid wolves. They have a definite foulness about them, and they looked starved."

Tark grabbed up an armful of fallen brush. "That does not bode well for us. They are not likely to relent, till they get a meal."

Delvar growled. "They will have to find their meal elsewhere."

"Agreed. Let's strengthen our defenses in hopes that they will find an easier meal than us." Tark grabbed at the fallen brush around the camp, and together they dragged and piled the brush and fallen trees, forming a thicker wall. They chopped down low-lying brush and anything that could be burned, and piled it along the barricade, making it as big as they could. Obi tried to calm his nerves. If they were overrun by these foul wolves, Vestos and Tug would be an easy meal.

Twenty-One

I regret nothing from my life, except the pain.

Layna took Tark by the arm. "The wolves will attack again. I have a suggestion. We need to be bigger."

Tark looked exhausted, his tone short. "Bigger? What do you mean?"

Layna readjusted her stance, pushing her arms straight up. In a loud voice, she said, "We need to be big and loud. We need to intimidate these wolves."

He snorted and shook his head.

It was clear to Obi that Tark didn't want any more of this foolishness, and Obi suspected that Layna could see that too. As to her plan, Obi thought it had merit and surprise on its side.

She pointed a finger at Tark. "Listen, can you hear how those wolves are snarling and growling? They are on the hunt. We are prey to them, nothing to fear."

Tark scanned the darkness, before turning back to Layna. "So we need to make sure they see us as more than an easy meal."

Layna smiled. "That's right. We need to be bigger and louder."

"The fire works pretty well for that," Tark mused.

She shook her head. "I think the firewood will be gone before the wolves decide to leave. We need to be large, loud, and scary. Like when Delvar came back to camp, and you charged up. You made that war cry."

"Okay, I see your point." Tark scratched his chin whiskers. "Not just hold them back but drive them off."

She smiled. "That is exactly what I mean."

Delvar raised an eyebrow. "So a war cry will do it?"

Layna corrected, "More than that. It has to be long, loud, and fierce. We need to be seen as a scary predator. We need to throw rocks, scream and holler, and become a predator in their eyes."

Tark nodded. "Something has to give. We can't stay awake for another night."

Obi stepped close to their conversation. "We need to get more wood."

Layna patted his shoulder. "And one more thing. We need to set fire to our fence and maybe the forest or at least some fallen trees."

Tark coughed. "What the hell? A forest fire is your plan? You are one crazy woman!"

Obi felt the knot in his stomach tighten. The fence was the only thing keeping the wolves out of their camp. "I don't like this idea. If we set fire to our fence, we have no wood to keep it going. The fire will be out in an hour."

Delvar shook his head is silent defiance.

Tark didn't like it either. "An hour's worth of defense by burning up all our barriers? If we conserve, the fire will last another five or six hours." Tark put up his hands, staring at Obi, then at Layna. "Let me think a moment."

Layna nodded. "That is why we have to do it now. In six hours those hairless jackals will still be out there, and we won't have this plan to consider."

Obi still didn't like it, but she made a good point. Every minute the group delayed meant a smaller fire; already those wolves were coming closer.

Tark announced, "Those wolves are not afraid of a fire contained, where their prey dance around it. Like you said, Delvar, the fire is a dinner bell."

Shocked and dismayed, Delvar scoffed, "This is madness to burn our defenses."

Tark raised his hand for him to be silent. "This is the best plan and our only plan."

Layna patted Delvar's arm. "Trust me. It will work. Obi and I can throw rocks—with a little luck, start a rock slide. At least it will seem like we are in more than one place."

Tark nodded to Layna. "When do we start?"

Layna picked up a makeshift torch and tossed it into the dry branches of the wall. "Now."

Tark let out a guttural battle cry, "Fire in our bellies!"

Delvar and Tannon roared with a fierceness that made Obi shake. He wanted to do something. The only thing he could think of was *Kiai* … "*Kiai*! *Kiai*!"

Tannon picked up a handful of stones. Yelling like a madman, he tossed them into the darkness. Layna made a hawklike screeching, long and loud.

The once-growling wolves' ears perked up by the sudden noises. Their growling changed to short growls mixed with barking and yips.

Obi picked up the largest rock he could throw over the barricade. Landing into the darkness, making a thump, it began rolling down the hill. Thumping and crashing rocks sent the pink creatures scattering out of its way.

Layna pulled a torch from the fire and made her way along the barricade, setting it on fire.

The party made a thunderous roar, the wall behind them making their voices louder.

Tark, using his shield to scoop up cherry-red coals of the fire, charged the fence line. Tark threw the coals into the air, making a shower of sparks rain down. He let loose his battle cry, "Fire in our bellies!"

The wolves skirted the barricade, turning this way and that way, trying to find a way through the burning barrier. Their growls had become fewer, the yips and barks more prevalent.

Layna yelled out, "That's it! They are beginning to break!"

Delvar threw a piece of wood—three feet long, hot with coals—into the darkness, making a guttural war cry and yelling curses. The flaming branch landed on a wolf, making it yelp and run into the darkness with its tail between its legs.

Tannon threw rock after rock, not caring where they landed, just that it added to the confusion. The left side of the fence line was engulfed in flames and a crackling, popping roar. A shower of skyward sparks danced into the mist. The right and the center were engulfed into a large bright flame, which grew larger and larger, until a roaring fire blazed. The intense heat drove the party away from the fire.

Yelping with confusion, the wolves retreated into the darkness. One by one the green eyes winked out.

Layna yelled out, "We are doing it! The wolves are retreating!"

Tark, Tannon, and Delvar yelled their cries of victory. Layna and Obi did too, taking time to throw rocks at the receding wolves. Tark let out a hoarse laugh. "Damn it, Layna. That was a great idea!"

Obi breathed a sigh of relief and laughed. The wolves were running away. His group would not get eaten today. It felt real good to laugh, and it was nice to hear Delvar and Tannon laughing together. "Tark, we're safe! We did it!"

Layna let out a giggle and hugged Tannon.

Tannon hugged her back. "That was clever! I told you that my sister is smart."

Delvar rolled his hand across his mustache. "And beautiful."

Tannon paused, considering Delvar's remark.

Obi thought Tannon would have a fit or get sullen or something, but he didn't.

Tannon gave Delvar a nod and smiled broadly. "Layna, you are beautiful and smart. You get your smarts and your good looks from me."

She rolled her eyes and kissed him on the cheek. "You were very brave and fierce."

Tark nudged Tannon. "That is quite a roar you have. You should use that more often. That's when the tide turned for us."

Tannon laughed. "Really, Tark? Your war cry was 'Fire in our bellies.'"

He shrugged. "The only thing I could think of."

The barrier burned bright and hot, crackling and popping, sending out sparks skyward. Everyone moved away till their backs were against the Dragonwall base. Tark, Delvar, and Tannon leaned against the wall, talking and slapping each other on the back, relieved and happy to be safe.

Layna cocked her head to one side. She shielded her eyes from the fire, like she was trying to peek over. "Shh, I hear something!"

Obi wondered how she could hear anything at all over the crackling fire and the laughter. Curious, he asked, "What do you hear?"

She scolded him. "Shh."

Tannon shook his head. "It's the fire. It hisses and pops. You know that."

She shot him a look. "Don't you hear it? There is a grumbling or a whisper."

Tannon cocked his ears. "I hear nothing—wait, there is something."

Obi mimicked Layna, blocking the firelight and trying to peek over. Initially he couldn't see anything but the flames. Shielding the flames with his hands, it was like peeking over. The firelight lit up the hillside; the Dragonwall was cast in an eerie red color, disappearing into the mist. Out in front Obi could make out the dark shadows of fallen trees. Just at the edge of the light, a row of green sparks lined the area, but they weren't sparks. They were the reflection of the pink hairless wolves' eyes. Some were lying down; others sat. They were all watching. Obi felt sick to his stomach, as a knot formed, tightly coiling. "The wolves are waiting for us."

Layna ignored him and cocked her head to one side. "Can you make that out, Tannon? It is saying something, like a poem."

Tannon leaned forward. "A meeting, or initial meeting, and wolves."

"Puppy," she corrected.

Tannon continued. "No, it's a rhyme. Not initial meeting, a fresh meeting and puppies."

Tark shrugged. "Talking is good. If they want a meet, I look forward to accommodating them."

Her face drained of color, Layna gasped. "It is puppies, and it is a rhyme, but it isn't about a meeting."

Tark waited. "What is it? I can hear it, but I can't make it out. Is that elvish?"

"Not elvish, more like ancient elvish or a dialect that hasn't been spoken in a thousand years. It is difficult to translate." She cocked her head to listen.

A lump caught in Obi's throat. A language that hadn't been spoken in a thousand years—it was the language during the Dragon Wars, the same time when the Dragonwall was built. Obi wanted to say something, but his voice caught in his throat.

Tark shot her a dark look. "Get on with it, Layna. What does it say?"

Layna said clearly, "The rhyme says, 'Fresh meat, fresh meat, fresh meat for the puppies to eat.'"

Obi swallowed hard. "Meat? What meat? Oh, we are the meat? They are waiting for the fires to die down, and they will come eat us!"

Layna patted him on the shoulder. "I wonder if they had this planned all along."

The whispering was getting louder. Although Obi couldn't understand the language, it sounded happy and cheerful, like a child's rhyme. "Whoever is whispering is controlling those wolves."

Tark cleared his throat. "The fires are getting lower, and we don't have any more wood."

The whispering grew louder, in a thickly accented voice that resonated through the air. "*Fresh meat, fresh meat, fresh meat for the puppies to eat.*"

Layna peeked her head up, shielding her eyes from their flaming barrier. "The rhyme has stopped."

Obi looked out into the dark and could see that the green baleful eyes had closed in. Their pink snouts and drooling jaws could be seen on the other side of the barrier.

One of the hairless wolves came close enough that Tannon loosed an arrow. The arrow hissed into the darkness. A solid thump resounded, so the arrow sank into its side. It leaped high into the air, letting out a growling snarl. It stumbled when it landed. Like the ghouls near the church, its fellow wolves fell on it in an instant and tore it to pieces, devouring their wounded companion.

Obi cringed at the sight. "That's the way. If they eat enough of each other, they will have no stomach for us."

Layna pointed to the remaining hairless creatures. "I think you are about to find out, Obi."

The hairless wolf had already been consumed, leaving nothing but a few stark-white bones. Those that did not get any turned hungrily toward their group. The scent of fresh blood seemed to embolden the wolves, for they could clearly be seen in the firelight. They circled and paced along the burning fence.

Tannon drew back his bow and shot another arrow. Even as he did, the other wolves crouched and leaped at the barrier, sending a shower of sparks into the air and across the ground.

Obi moved forward, stabbing at a dog that had crashed into the fence. He could hear the others shouting and cursing, as they too fought wolves tangled in the barricade. "Survive this attack," Obi said to himself. "It will be enough to drive them off."

Obi attacked with all the strength his exhausted body could muster. He stabbed the dog in front of him deeply in the chest. It snarled and snapped its great jaws at the haft of the spear, catching it momentarily as Obi tried to jerk it back. To his left another dog had leaped the barrier. Layna rushed forward with drawn sickles to meet it.

Obi stabbed again at the wounded dog, striking it in the neck. It slumped toward the ground but was held up by the tangle of brush it was caught in. Obi looked over at Layna as the other dog pounced. In a whirl of blades, Layna deftly rolled under the dog's leap. The animal paid a heavy price for its rash attack. Layna severed a forepaw with one sickle and disemboweled it with the second. It landed and stumbled, crashing into the nearby fire. The dog's momentum caused several burning logs to be knocked out of the fire and sent rolling down the slope. One burning log came to rest against Tug, who began twitching violently and crying out. The dog Layna had killed thrashed a moment in the fire itself, before it collapsed, its bloody viscera dousing much of the remaining fire in a horrible stench.

Layna turned away from the barrier, but her ankle gave out. With a soft crunch, she fell to her knees; she cried out in pain.

Obi turned back to the menace at the fence. Two more wolves leaped the barrier. Obi stabbed hard at the one charging him. He caught the wolf midleap; the tremendous impact drove the spear through the wolf's body and out its back. The twitching dog fell to the side, tearing the spear from his hands. Obi scrambled away from the second dog. He fumbled with the hilt of a short sword at his belt. A dog leaped at him, snapping its jaws at him. The two of them crashed in a heap down the slope.

The wolf bit at Obi, only to get a large mouthful of his robe. Obi stuck a thumb into an eye of the dog and rolled, curling his feet up. When the wolf opened its mouth to bite again, Obi kicked out with both feet, sending it flying into the fence.

Obi rolled again and got to his feet, scrambling madly for Tug's short sword that he had dropped.

Layna had crawled to Tug and removed the burning log. Delvar was engaged with two wolves at once, as Tark pulled his sword from another.

Obi took a step toward the side of the barrier to again defend that position.

Layna screamed, "OBI! Behind you!"

Instinctively Obi ducked. A great club, aimed for his head, hit his right shoulder. His right arm exploded in pain; the force knocked him to the ground. He needed that short sword; he rolled away to see what attacked him.

Stunned with fear and awe, Obi looked up. Standing right over him was an enormous troll-like woman. She stood taller than Vestos with huge hands and bare feet with sharp claws. She held a large crude club in one hand and swung it with a strength that belied her bony limbs. She smashed the club into the ground where Obi had been a moment before.

Bent over from the force of her own blow, Obi looked right into her face, as she snarled at him. She had horrible rancid breath, orange teeth, large eyes, and an oversize nose. Besides the twisted features and disfigurement, Obi was shocked to see how much the troll woman reminded him of Majora.

The troll woman raised the club over her head to smash Obi. He rolled to his right. He called out, "Help, help!"

The club smashed into the rocks next to Obi, cutting him with chips and fragments of broken stone. Obi feinted to the right and rolled toward the troll woman.

Rather than use the club, the large troll stomped down on Obi with her clawed feet. The crunch of his lower leg sent a sharp, shrill pain through him. He screamed. The clawed talons dug into his thigh, dragging him to the ground.

Obi thrashed, trying to free himself, but realized he was pinned under the troll woman's massive clawed feet.

Delvar charged up, brandishing his long sword. She spun to face him, shifting her weight, grinding Obi's broken bones into the hard-packed gravel. The grinding bones sent a wave of nausea and torrid pain through both legs. Obi cried out in anguish.

Delvar moved in, slashing. The troll woman rocked back, bringing the club heavily to the ground, sending another shower of rock chips. Every movement sent more pain raging through Obi's legs. He wished Delvar would kill her or that the troll would kill him, to put him out of his misery.

A large rock about the size of Obi's head had been unearthed and rolled against his side. Obi grabbed it. Using his pain to fuel the attack, he smashed the rock into the troll's ankle.

The troll woman twisted to meet Delvar. Pain roared through Obi, sending his legs into spasms. The club whistled through the air, smashing the side of Obi's head. There was a brilliant flash of light as the blow connected. Obi found himself staring out at ground level at the paws of two more wolves approaching. The happy little rhyme had started again, calling the puppies to the fresh meat. Darkness was creeping over him; he realized he was slipping into unconsciousness and surely death. Delvar fell in front of his view. His eyes were closed, and blood streamed from his scalp. The cold blackness covered Obi; in the distance Layna screamed.

Twenty-Two

Swimming in the blackness.

Surely he was dead, swimming in the blackness. Muffled at the very edge of his ability to hear were voices. Obi could not think as to whose they were or where he might be. He remembered the pain and the force of the troll woman's club. Most of all he remembered how much the troll woman had looked like Majora. Yes, it was Majora. She had tricked them, shape-shifting into one of her swamp people, to catch them at the foot of the wall. Obi felt a rushing panic swell inside of him.

He recalled hearing Majora's cackling laugh and how she had crushed his legs, sending searing pain through him. He could feel his bones rubbing back and forth against the other. Majora had stomped on him with her cruel feet.

Obi tried to see if any of his friends were still alive, but it was so dark, and he could not move or even lift his head. He heard another voice but could not understand what it said. He blinked, trying to see through the darkness. He managed to open his eyes, and Majora, the troll woman, stood there with a menacing smile and let out a loud, cackling laugh. Obi was bound to a large pile of timbers. She was planning to roast him, just like a boar.

She rolled two fingers together; yellow streams of magical energy moved down her fingers. A soft pop came, which turned into a bright yellow flame that caught the logs on fire. The fire grew quickly; the bits of rope that bound him were beginning to smolder. Obi struggled to get loose, but the ropes were too tight. He was trapped.

Majora, the troll, let out a soft chuckling, as she fed logs to the fire. The flame steadily grew larger. She bent close, till he could feel her breath on his cheek. Her face was covered with rough gray warts; her nose and chin were longer than before, and her teeth had been filed to sharp points. Her hair was tangled with pond weed and small bones. She grinned at him, showing her sharp teeth. She licked her lips with a long black tongue. "I mustn't touch the scribe. You're not done yet."

In the firelight, he could see his friends. Layna and Tannon were bound with ropes. Tug and Vestos were torn apart, and there was no sign of the others. He hoped they got away. Outside the firelight, the green-eyed wolves lay waiting for their meal.

Majora reached for his face. "I should wait. Yet I'm so hungry, perhaps a nibble."

Obi tried to pull away but couldn't. He cried out in fear, as she came close, licking her lips. Her tongue felt cold and wet. She pushed back his hair. "I am going to nibble off your face!"

Obi thrashed back and forth, trying desperately to get out of his bonds. "HELP! Help!"

A gentle hand pulled a washcloth along his brow. Obi opened his eyes.

Layna sat next to him, her hand on his forehead and the other gently shaking his arm. "Obi, you are having a bad dream. You're okay. You're safe."

Obi jumped. "How did you get out?"

Layna smiled at him reassuringly. "What? You were dreaming."

Obi glanced around the dimly lit room, searching for Majora, the troll woman. "What happened? How did we escape Majora?"

"Escape Majora?" Layna looked at him quizzically. "Obi, Majora saved us!"

"What? No, she was the troll! She tricked us!"

Layna laughed softly. "No, Obi. Majora saved us from the troll! She and the swamp people saved everyone!"

Obi tried to see more of the structure. Large beams of wood ran along the roofline. No windows just a double door. Straw covered the floor, and cots lay along the walls. "Are we in Majora's barn?"

Layna wrung out the rag and dabbed his head. "Yes, for some time now. You have been running a fever."

Beyond Layna, he saw Tug and Vestos, lying in similar cots. He shifted to see Layna better, but the throbbing pain in his shoulder and leg stopped him. He groaned. His right arm was in a sling; the right side of his face was puffy and sore. His left leg stuck out from under the blanket, and was bound in cloth and sticks, running from knee to ankle.

Layna assured him. "Easy, Obi. You are safe but not yet well. Rest and I will tell you what happened. What do you remember last?"

Obi thought for a moment. "Is everyone all right? How are Vestos and Tug?"

"Everyone is okay. Vestos and Tug are fine too."

From two cots down, Vestos rolled up on his elbow. His voice cracked when he spoke. "I feel like the wrong end of a mule."

Layna gasped. "You're awake!"

Tug moved a little and moaned. He opened one eye. "Vestos, you still look like shit."

Obi was happy to see both of them alive. He relaxed a little. "The last thing I can recall, I was stomped on by the troll, seeing Delvar fall in front of me, all covered in blood."

Vestos rolled to his side and moaned. He told Tug, "You are not looking any better."

Tug weakly glanced at him. "If I look half as bad as you, I would be dead a week!"

Layna moved to prop a pillow for him. "You both need to rest easy now, and all of you have been running a fever from the ghoul poison."

Vestos and Tug slumped back down into their cots. Tug grumbled out, "The last thing I recall was we were attacked by ghouls and fighting off that captain from the wall."

Layna raised an eyebrow. "We didn't fight Captain Jacobs. You dreamed that."

"I don't recall anything except being damn cold and wet," Vestos confessed.

Obi smiled. "Perhaps, Layna, you should start at the church."

She patted his good hand and smiled. "Let's see, the church."

Obi could tell that Tug didn't believe that their group didn't fight Captain Jacobs, by the way he was grumbling. He half listened to Layna explain their escape from the church and how it was an accident that the church had burned down, and so they had run to the river and crossed, stumbling in the dark, and how they found the rope was cut.

Tug let out a raspy laugh. "See? That captain is an ass."

Layna patted Tug on the shoulder and continued her story. She left out everyone being irritated with Delvar. "So, anyway, after that, I got the log off Tug and threw it back on the fire. I turned and saw this enormous figure standing over Obi. I yelled to warn him, but it was too late."

Obi stammered out, "Not too late, I am sure you saved my life."

She continued her story. "I collected my sickles and did my best to get the fire together, but there was no time. More goblin dogs were coming over the barricade."

Obi asked, "Goblin dogs? I thought them hairless wolves."

Layna continued, "Majora calls them goblin dogs. They aren't really dogs, like we know. They are evil things that serve evil masters, like the Hag."

Obi tried to sit up, but his leg protested. "Is that the troll woman?"

"Yes, Majora says that she was once a human witch who had been corrupted by her own evil spells and dealings with things not of this world. She is known as the Dragon Hag or just the Hag," she explained.

Obi readjusted his position, propping a pillow under his head. "Dragon Hag? That seems like an appropriate name for her. I got to smell her breath."

"Anyway, the Hag is the master of the goblin dogs. It was our bad luck that she was out hunting. Her dogs picked up our scent."

Obi raised his good hand. "With our wounded, I bet we were easy tracking."

She smiled at him. "That is what Tark said too. Majora says that the Hag loves to torture people and then eat them alive. No way were we going to get away, once the Hag was on our scent."

Obi swallowed hard. He could feel his heart quicken, and the short hairs on his neck began to rise. "How are we not dead? How did we get away? How?"

She shushed him. "We had put up a good fight against the dogs, but with the Hag taking down you and Delvar, it left just Tark, Tannon, and me. By this time, Tannon was out of arrows, and I could barely stand. The Hag and her dogs had us backed up against the wall, and things were looking very grim."

"I can imagine. So, what happened?"

Layna waited a moment and then beamed. "That was when the swamp people began dropping down the wall."

"Swamp people can climb?"

She nodded vigorously. "They were amazing! They climbed down the wall like spiders and dropped right in the midst of the Hag and her dogs. The swamp people are the most frighteningly ferocious things I have ever seen. The fight at the foot of the wall was short and brutal. The dogs were no match for the swamp people. When the Hag saw that she could not win, she and her dogs ran off with their tails between their legs."

"The Hag wasn't killed?" Obi asked.

"Oh, no. She is still out there. Majora says that she never comes over the wall. She knows that it's too dangerous. If the soldiers were to see her, she would be hunted down. Majora says that she is clever and devious but a through-and-through coward."

Obi interrupted, "How did we get over the wall, and how did we get here?"

Layna grinned mischievously. "If you'll stop talking, I could tell you."

Obi couldn't wait to hear more of the adventure. He clamped his hand over his mouth and muffled out, "Please continue."

She smiled. "So after the Hag and her dogs were run off, Majora lowered a rope to us, and, with the help of the swamp people, she had us pulled up the wall. Tark and Tannon stayed at the bottom of the wall to the very last, tying up slings for the rest of us. Then they hauled us up."

Filled with disbelief, Obi scoffed, "They hauled us up and across the forest and swamp?"

She nodded. "Almost effortlessly the swamp people carried us to the forest. We rested, and the swamp people guarded. While I was asleep, they made litters and carried everyone except Majora, Tannon, and Tark back to Majora's Island."

Obi said, "That is amazing! How long have we been unconscious?"

"Three days. Majora used some magic and some herbs to keep you that way. She said that, by keeping you and the others unconscious, the trip would be easier on you and faster for us."

Obi shook his head in disbelief. "The last thing I was thinking about before the Hag knocked me out was how she resembled Majora and that we were going to die by her hand."

A loud cackling laugh sounded at the door.

This was not the happy cackle that Obi had known but a more menacing Majora. Startled, Obi stiffly turned.

Majora stood in the doorway of the barn. Her arms were crossed, and she was tapping one foot in annoyed agitation. "Ho, ho, and I thought you liked me!"

Obi swallowed hard. "Eh—"

Majora raised her arms in a flourish.

Expecting to be cursed, Obi winced.

Majora began to laugh. "Ha! Gotcha! My dear boy, it's quite all right. You and your friends have been through a lot. No harm done."

Tug called out, "Told you, Obi! She was sweet on you."

Majora, half surprised, said, "You two are awake? How do you feel?"

Tug grumbled, and Vestos shrugged.

"Hmm, too soon. Layna, would you mind fetching me two cups of the black tea?"

Layna nodded and quickly exited the barn.

Majora came close to Vestos, waving a thin twig over him, then over Tug. "Yes, both of you need some more rest—about five days, I imagine. You are doing well. It takes some time to recover from the ghoul's sickness."

Layna returned with two wooden cups. "It was the end of the pot."

Majora took them and sprinkled a bit of salt over them. She gave a cup to Vestos and Tug. She pointed to Layna to help Tug sit up. "Drink this down. It will help with the chills and will sustain you until that poison is out."

Weakly they drank the tea. Vestos shuddered once; Tug coughed before drinking it all down.

Majora continued, "You two rest easy."

As quickly as Layna gathered up the cup from each, they were sleeping and looked more restful.

Majora came to Obi's side and patted his cheek.

Obi could see mischief in her eyes and looked relieved. "Well, eh, I was dreaming."

With a lecherous grin she said, "I am so glad to hear you were dreaming about me!"

Obi bowed his head sheepishly. "Majora, I am sorry I thought ill of you."

"Not to worry, lad. Nearly everyone is suspicious of the swamp witch. Although I can't imagine why."

Layna turned to go. "I'll let you two talk. I'm going to see what my brother and Tark are doing."

Obi waited till Layna had closed the door behind her. "Thank you, Majora, for saving us. I really thought that we were going to die."

"You nearly did, although I must take some responsibility. I got to thinking that perhaps I did not emphasize how dangerous it is over the wall. I fussed about it for a day and then thought, I should be nearby, if something goes awry. I knew there was a problem when you did not make it back by the third night. So I asked for help from my swamp friends. We were waiting for nightfall to cross the wall."

Obi exclaimed, "Wait for night! You said to never be over the wall at night."

"I said for YOU to never be over the wall at night. The swamp people do not like how open the land is over the Dragonwall. They would not go during the day. I needed their help, so we waited till night."

"You can talk to the swamp people? I didn't think they spoke."

She cocked her head back and forth, as if trying to reduce her words to something Obi could understand. "We came to an understanding."

"Please thank them for us, if you can."

She patted his cheek, giving it a squeeze. "I surely will."

Obi had forgotten until now why they had gone over the Dragonwall. "Majora! The box. Was it the one that you wanted?"

"Yes, it is. I had hoped there would be more than just the few scrolls in that box, but it was enough."

"That's what was in it, scrolls?"

"Yes. Do you mean to say, as curious as you are, you didn't look inside the box?"

"Well, there wasn't really any time. Once we had found the box and set off the trap, we needed to leave. Then the ghouls and we were fighting to get back."

Majora shook her head. "Remarkable. You really went into the forsaken lands, not for treasure, but in hopes to see a dragon."

"I think Tug and Delvar would have preferred treasure, but my Sovereign asked me to find the truth of dragons. Are they real or a myth? I still don't know."

"Trust me, dragons exist. My dear boy, dragons are much more dangerous than the things you have only barely survived. I fear that, if you encounter a dragon, it may be the last thing you learn."

"I believe you, Majora, but I truly would like to see a dragon."

She smiled down at him. "If you do see one, I would not be surprised if you change your mind about the wisdom of seeking one out."

"I suppose, but I think I would rather be afraid for a little while than live a life wondering *what if?*"

She threw her head back, letting out a loud cackle. "Oh dear, you have the worst case of curiosity that I have ever seen! My magic and herbs can mend your bones, but, this other illness, I have no cure for that."

Obi was certain Majora was teasing him. He shifted, trying to get up. "I didn't see a dragon, so that will have to wait. Could I see the scrolls we brought back?"

She patted him on his good shoulder. "To answer, yes, you may look at the scrolls, but I doubt they will mean anything to you. The language they are written in is very old. For now you should rest. Your wounds have not mended, and there will be time."

"Can you read the scrolls?"

Majora stood up, wagging a finger at him. "First things first, you need to rest. In a few days we will look at the scrolls together. In the meantime, write in your journal and sleep."

"My journal! You have it? I thought it might be lost!"

"I knew that this was important to you. I made sure it came back." She pulled Obi's journal from the satchel that hung over her shoulder and handed it to him. "Here are your quills and ink, and a few pieces of charcoal."

"Thank you. I will write and rest as you say."

Majora nodded and smiled. "Rest first."

Twenty-Three
The end of the beginning.

Every morning Layna would show up with a large bowl of porridge, sweetened with honey and spiced with Majora's herbs. Promptly after eating, Obi would spend time writing in his journal and drawing pictures of the things he had seen across the Dragonwall. During the day, he rested often and slept. Occasionally he would check on Vestos and Tug, but Layna would encourage him back to bed. Convinced they are in capable hands, Obi would return to his cot.

On the eighth day, Majora showed up with a twisted, gnarled piece of wood with cloth wrapped around the Y portion. "This is a crutch. It is time you came out and ate with the rest of us."

Obi was exhausted from lying in bed for so long and relished the idea of getting up; most of all he wanted to look at the scrolls and the box.

Majora showed him how to use the crutch, setting the Y under his arm and taking the weight off his hurt leg.

Obi took a few steps and hopped on his good leg, getting his balance. "This is harder than you made it look."

Majora seemed pleased. "You will be running around here in no time."

Obi wiped his brow. "I am out of shape!"

Majora nodded. "It is the ghoul poison. You're sweating it out. Your broken leg bones are easy to mend, but the ghoul scratches are more sinister."

"Is that why Vestos and Tug are still sleeping?"

Majora patted his arm, smiling at him. It wasn't her normal lecherous grin but a look of pride. "You have been doing more than drawing in your book."

Obi readjusted his crutch. "Just thinking about the ghouls."

"Yes, the ghouls are dangerous. The ghouls over the Dragonwall are more so. They are infected with a vile magic."

"What kind of vile magic? What does it do?"

"This magic came about during the Dragon War, to keep up an undead army. This is a sinister magic. If a person survived the attack, they are destined to become a ghoul."

"So Tug and Vestos were close to turning?"

Her mischievous smile returned. "Most of your party was headed that way. Don't worry. I managed to cure everyone of the ghoul disease. Tug and Vestos were close to changing. Their recovery will take longer than your leg to mend. Now enough of this. Come on outside. Breakfast is waiting."

The sun had risen into a cloudless sky. Obi guessed it was midmorning. The bright sun made his eyes tear, but the sunshine felt good across his skin.

Layna came away from the fire, holding a bowl of porridge. She walked without a limp. "It is about time you made it to breakfast."

Obi smiled. "Thank you. Your ankle is doing better?"

She set the bowl across from him. She put her leg up on the table, waggling her foot up and down. "Good as new. You just missed Delvar, Tark, and Tannon. They went out hunting."

Majora came out of the barn and headed into her house. Obi couldn't help but wonder when he would see the scrolls.

By the next morning Obi was happy to see Tug and Vestos making their way out of the barn and having breakfast with the group. He could see that Tug and Vestos were still weak, but their color had returned and the dark circles under their eyes were gone. Tug still had darkened fingernails, which made Obi a little nervous. Vestos did not seem to mind the regular attention of everyone, especially Layna and Majora. Obi suspected Vestos was playing up the sympathy for some added attention. Layna and Majora didn't seem to mind.

Obi hobbled around the little island, trying to help out where he could. Mostly this turned out to be tending the fire and cooking. He was saddened when Tark and Tannon went into the swamp to hunt; Obi was sure they were seeing all sorts of interesting things. When they came back, they would pass the time by describing what they saw, usually as they sat around the evening campfire. Obi enjoyed these times, and the events over the Dragonwall began to seem less and less frightful.

"Now that you're up and around, Vestos, when are we going to start trying some of that gruel?"

Vestos was happy to start his normal morning routine. "Tonight I will soak the grains. And since we have some honey, it will be very tasty."

Majora placed the box beside Obi. She opened the lid. "Here you go. Take a look at these scrolls."

The scrolls were made of velum and had yellowed with time. They were dry and rough and felt as strong as leather. They were written in a spidery, flowing script, which seemed to convey a hint of cruelty in its elegant letters. As Majora had predicted, Obi had no idea what the writing said.

Majora pointed to a word. "This one means *empire*. That one is *slave*."

Obi tried to decipher any basics to the language. He thought he would start with cataloging the variety of letters. He pulled out his notebook and began copying the scroll.

Majora pointed to a few more words, telling him of their meaning.

"Well, it isn't much to go on, but it is a start," Obi concluded.

Majora explained, "This form of writing was what had been used by the slaves of the dragons centuries ago."

"Dragons have slaves who write?"

Majora stifled a cackle. "Obi, you have to remember that the empire of the dragons was really quite large. And presumably is so to this day."

"I didn't think of dragons as having empires. I thought they were more like animals that had great size."

Majora raised a finger. "That is the sort of thinking the leads to the end of many dragon hunters. They think that they are after an oversize bear and treat it as such. A dragon is a powerful, intelligent creature, convinced of its own superiority. They are master manipulators, leaders, and spell-users. They often have many servants, both willing and unwilling. Never underestimate how dangerous a dragon can be. The dragon lords had cities of slaves and servants that worshiped them like gods."

Obi found the idea of people worshiping dragons interesting. "Dragons have cities?"

Majora nodded with certainty. "Dragon lords had a large government, and someone needed to keep records, like this scroll before you."

"Do you mean that dragons can read?"

Majora laughed. "Are you not listening? Read and write too! Who do you think invented this form of writing?"

"How could something as large as a dragon write?" he mused.

Majora shook her head. "Size has nothing to do with it. Dragons may be large, but their hands and feet are shaped like yours. They don't have paws, like a bear. I have heard that they can grasp things, just as we can. They could wield a sword, if they wanted, but would never choose to use such a lesser weapon."

Obi remembered something in his journal and gasped. Quickly he pulled it out and flipped through the pages. "At the time I was scouting for water, I thought I had found an odd-looking mud puddle. A ghoul was smashed in the bottom of it, and the water was tainted."

Majora arched an eyebrow. "And you drew this puddle?"

"At the time I thought nothing of it, but perhaps it means more than I realized." Obi opened the page where he had drawn the body of the ghoul in the odd-shaped mud puddle. "Majora, look at this!"

As they looked again at the picture, Obi described what he had seen and added to the picture to show what he meant. The body was in a pool the shape of a clawed handprint, as if the ghoul had been crushed into the earth by a huge hand. Majora and Obi stared at one another.

Majora let out a loud cackling laugh. "My boy, it seems you might have been closer to a dragon than you realized."

Obi felt a rush of excitement. "Do you really think that was a dragon track?"

She wagged her finger under his nose. "I don't like the look in your eye, Obi!"

Obi stared at the page. "The puddle was five or six feet across."

"Your eyes brighten like a child, but you don't forget what Majora tells you. Dragons are dangerous! If there be a dragon nearby, it did not miss noticing you. You were merely too insignificant to be bothered with. Just like you ignore a bird as you walk along."

"I bet the dragon smashed it like someone would a rat!"

Majora sighed. "Perhaps. Perhaps not. Be truly careful with this obsession of yours, Obi. Like any creature, if you pester a dragon, it will bite you or stomp on you, like that ghoul. My herbs won't cure that!"

Obi's smile grew. "What? I thought you said the swamp has plants that will cure anything!"

Majora shook her finger again in mock severity. "And it does! I just might not choose to share them with one so stubborn!"

Obi was guessing Majora was joking, but he really couldn't be certain exactly how much joking and how much truth she spoke.

She added, "If you decide to continue your quest to find a dragon, perhaps you can retrieve another scroll for me. It is located in the great elven library at Midreach."

Obi liked that idea of traveling on top of the Dragonwall. He might be able to see a dragon and still be safe atop the wall. He would have to bring up the idea to Tark.

Obi made his way back to the barn with the dry straw and cots. Tark, Vestos, and Tug lay on their cots. Delvar, who had received a terrific blow from the Hag, had already recovered. He had enjoyed having some lighthearted fun with the more seriously wounded. "You do realize, if it were not for my superior hardiness and good armor, I might be laid up with you men."

Obi scratched his head. "Really?"

Tug shook his head. "No, Delvar is ribbing us."

Delvar rolled his hand across his mustache, turning his movement into a large flexing pose. "I am made from oak trees and iron nails, and nothing can keep me down long."

Tug rolled his eyes. "Perhaps we should learn to be as showy as Delvar. That way we can look more wounded and be ignored in a fight."

Everyone laughed; Delvar did too.

The men had settled down, and their conversations went quiet. Obi approached Delvar. "That night when the Hag was attacking us, you came to help me. I want to say thank-you. She would have killed me, if you hadn't attacked her. You risked your life to save mine."

Delvar opened his mouth, then closed it. He looked stunned.

Obi could see that Delvar was clearly uncomfortable, and his ears turned red. Obi pondered that, underneath the bolstering and merry-making, Delvar was quite shy. Obi grinned at Delvar and didn't wait. Obi turned and exited the barn.

Majora was moving quickly around, looking at this scroll, to the next, and back again. She let out a small cackling laugh. "Ah, sniping and banter are good signs. Soon they are well enough to travel."

Obi felt torn by Majora's news, both happy and sad. He knew she was right. All of them were feeling better and becoming restless. They were ready to move on and see new things, but all had grown very fond of Majora. Obi would miss her.

The next day Obi had asked Tark about going to Midreach to follow the search for dragons. He agreed, and so did the rest of the party members. With a renewed sense of hope, and Majora's declaration of their health, the party was eager to have a large meal and a good night's rest before heading to Midreach.

By early morning, Tannon and Tark had tracked and brought in a large boar. Layna's owl brought in two fat rabbits, and Tug had caught two big catfish from Majora's moat.

Majora announced, "This is a good and plentiful bounty. We should feast to celebrate good fortune and new friends."

Obi busied himself around camp, gathering firewood, peeling roots, and stoking the fire for the boar.

Tug elbowed Obi. "Here, I will show you the best way for roasting catfish. I learned this as a boy."

Obi watched as Tug, using a thick dagger, deboned and fileted the catfish with skill that would match anyone's. "You learned this as a boy? Could you show me how to do that?"

He nodded. "Weren't you paying attention?"

"Well, you did do it so fast."

Tug laughed and pulled out a second catfish. "See? You start here."

Obi watched the steps. He doubted if he could remember them, but he watched anyway. He was happy to see Tug in such a good mood.

Vestos arrived with a large pot of rabbit stew, made with special herbs and spices, and placed it over the cook fire. Obi felt glad to be warm and surrounded by friends. They celebrated with eating and laughter. Sometime during the festivities, Layna and Delvar showed their skills at dancing and telling stories of the adventure.

Majora and Tark had the boar prepared and roasted. When it was done, they sent Obi and Tug with the roasted boar to the dock for the swamp people.

Majora called them all together one last time. "Tomorrow you leave for Midreach, and I wish you well on your journey."

There was a tone in Majora's words that Obi picked up on. It was a subtle tone, which reminded him of the rhyme the Hag had chanted, a subtle vibration of magic.

Majora continued, "May the lands that you travel, help you in your time of need. May you protect the land, when no others will." She threw a powder into the fire, and a bright flash and a huge cloud of smoke erupted. The air smelled strongly of roses.

Obi stifled a scream and changed it into a cough. He doubted anyone would notice.

Majora smiled and gave her best imitation of Tark. She clapped her hands "Off to bed. Take heed not to disturb the swamp people's dinner."

Obi thought the imitation was remarkable. "How did you do that?"

She looked Obi and grinned. "You are still on the menu."

Everyone laughed. With full stomachs and laughter, they headed for the barn. Tark looked at Obi. "You aren't going to cause trouble tonight, are you?"

Obi ducked his head and smiled. "No. Not tonight anyway."

Tark looked surprised and then laughed, shaking his head. "Well, good. I'm too full and too sleepy to thrash you tonight."

Obi lay down, and thought about getting up and looking at the swamp people. He thought about the things Majora had said about his curiosity and the trouble it could bring. He thought about the lessons that the Sovereign taught. Tonight Obi would hold his curiosity in check and keep his friends safe. He closed his eyes and, with a smile on his face, fell into a deep, dreamless sleep.

Epilogue

The spiritual link established, Majora could feel the Hag's anger.

The Hag sneered. "So, was it worth it, witch? You really have no idea what to do."

"Of course it was worth it. Oh, I do know what to do. After all, Hag, I haunt your dreams now."

"Ha, don't flatter yourself. Even now your every move helps me in the end. You usher in your destruction and everyone else's."

Majora could feel the Hag's frustration and turmoil. "Really, Hag? Who huddles in a dark hole, and who has the box of Kaloni and his scrolls?"

"Bah, you have scrolls that you cannot read. That means nothing, witch! Your ignorance will be your downfall!"

"And your arrogance will be yours!" Majora cut the spiritual link between herself and the Hag. It had been a gamble to contact her, but Majora had learned what she needed to know. The link confirmed what Majora had suspected, that crossing the wall damaged the magic that created it.

It was tied to the lost treaty between the Dragon lords and the southern alliance. Every time a human crossed the wall, a little of the magic was lost. It was this that had been eroding the power of the wall over the years. Majora had translated the scrolls of Kaloni and had learned many things. The most important of which was the blessing she had performed on the little party of adventurers a few days ago. Now they could cross the wall without damaging the forces that built it. It was a small thing, but the old swamp witch knew every change in the tide starts with a drop of water, and hers was on its way to Midreach.

The End

About the Authors

Dennis D. Montoya grew up in the state of Washington, and started gaming and writing short stories in high school. After two enlistments in the military, he went to college. He is happily married and works as a registered nurse. He enjoys photography, gaming, and spending quality time with his wife, Colleen.

H. C. "Hank" Strom grew up in Alaska, then attended high school and college in the state of Washington, where he now resides. He works for an electrical manufacturing company. He enjoys riding his motorcycle, and the company of his friends and family.

www.facebook.com/pages/Over-the-Dragonwall/760452244027217.

We look forward to hearing from you.